SWEENEY SISTERS SERIES

# tangle of
# strings

a novel

## ASHLEY
## FARLEY

*For women's fiction fans*

## ONE

ANNIE

Annie checked the clock on the dashboard. She had eight minutes to change into her work clothes, grab a snack, and still be on time for her after-school job at Captain Sweeney's Seafood Market. She turned off the main road and zoomed down the wooded driveway toward the house. When she rounded the last bend, she saw Heidi leaning against the hood of her vintage turquoise Mustang. Annie slammed on the brakes, her Honda Accord skidding sideways on the gravel. Her anger surged at the sight of those ridiculous cat's eye sunglasses her mother wore. Heidi's white blonde hair was piled high in a messy bun on top of her head, while hot-pink lipstick accented her dazzling smile. Who did she think she was? Was she auditioning for Sandy's role in a remake of the movie *Grease*? What was she doing here, anyway? Annie had asked Heidi repeatedly not to contact her. Couldn't she take a hint? Annie thought about running her over, and then realized that pelting her with a spray of gravel as she peeled out of the driveway might be a better choice. Heidi stepped in front of Annie's car preventing her from doing either. Not that she would have. She was not a violent person. Her mother just made her crazy.

Removing her house keys from her purse on the passenger seat, Annie jumped out of the car and marched toward the front door. "Please leave, Heidi. I told you I don't want to see you."

Heidi followed her up the brick steps. "I need to talk to you, Annie. Please. It will only take a few minutes."

"I don't have a few minutes," she said, fumbling to insert her key into the lock. "I'm late for work." Her heart pounding against her rib cage, Annie locked the bolt once inside and slumped back against the door. She forced herself to inhale deep gulps of air until her breathing slowed.

She walked down the hall to her bedroom where she changed into her work polo and blue jeans. She tied her honey-colored hair into a pert ponytail at the back of her head and slipped on her high-top black Chuck Taylors. Grabbing from her closet a hoodie the same shade of moss green as her polo, she went to the kitchen for a snack. She snatched a banana from the bowl of fruit on the counter and rummaged through the refrigerator for a drink, finally settling on one of Bitsy's juice boxes. She started for the front door, and then stopped in her tracks. So what if she was late for work. If she took her time, maybe Heidi would get tired of waiting and leave.

Leaning against the kitchen counter, she peeled her banana and pinched off a bite. She stared down at the miniature cockapoo, her cute little face eager for attention, in the doggy crate on the floor near her feet. "I'm sorry, Snowflake. I have to go to work. I don't have time to play with you."

Santa had given the puppy to her little sister for Christmas. Snowflake barked a lot, but everyone in the family loved her. The family that was Annie's in every way but name.

Annie stuffed the rest of the banana in her mouth and sucked all the apple juice out of the box through the tiny straw. She removed a dog biscuit from the glass jar on the counter, broke it in half, and fed it to Snowflake through the metal door. "Be a good girl, now." She stroked the puppy's silky ear with her finger through the mesh. "Bitsy will be home to play with you soon."

Straightening, Annie slipped on her hoodie and walked back through the house to the front door. Heidi, her jean jacket held tight against her midsection, waited for her at the bottom of the porch steps, blocking the way to Annie's car.

"Honey, please. I really need to talk to you. If you'll just give me a chance to explain."

Annie glared at her. "You gave up the right to call me honey, or any other term of endearment for that matter, when you abandoned me." She tried to brush past Heidi, but she grabbed her by the arm.

"That happened a long time ago. I was a different person then. I made a bad decision. But I'm trying to make it right now."

Annie yanked her arm away. "The decision was right for you at the time. A very selfish decision, I might add. You took off to Hollywood to chase your dreams of becoming a big movie star, and left me with a man who didn't know how to scramble an egg or balance his checkbook, let alone raise a little girl."

Heidi's cobalt eyes glistened with tears. "Was your life really that miserable, sweetheart? I didn't know—"

"Because you never bothered to find out." Annie clenched her fists. "At least Daddy loved me, which is more than I can say for you. But he wasn't a good provider. For the first time in my life, I don't have to worry about how I'm going to pay for groceries. Or who's going to cook dinner. The Sweeneys care about me. They ask me about my day. And help me with my geometry homework. Faith buys me new clothes. Bitsy loves having a big sister to take her places. Mike gave me a car for Christmas, for crying out loud." She flicked her wrist at the silver Honda Accord in the driveway. "Don't mess this up for me, Heidi. Just go away and leave me alone."

Annie stalked off toward her car, but Heidi teetered after her on spiked-heel booties. "You and I were getting along so well together back in December, before you found out who I was. We were becoming friends. We share so many things in common. I know we can build a life together based on that friendship. You can come live with me. I recently signed a lease on the second-floor apartment in a newly renovated old home down on Broad Street, on the Battery. I think you'll like it. I even have an extra bedroom for you."

"God! You're not listening to me." Annie said, her face scarlet with anger. "I told you I'm happy here. I don't want to move to Charleston. My life is here, in Prospect."

Annie moved to open her car door but Heidi blocked the way. "You'd love Charleston, if you'd give it a chance. There are so many great restaurants. The place is alive with college kids your age. I hope to start my own business, but I can't do it alone. I need you by my side." Heidi brushed a stray strand of hair off Annie's forehead. "You have to admit, it sounds appealing."

Annie slapped her hand away. "I'd rather die than work in the same kitchen with you."

"Please, baby. Don't be this way."

"I'm not your baby! You abandoned your baby sixteen years ago." Shoving Heidi out of the way, Annie jumped into her car and struggled to fasten her seat belt. As she shot off down the driveway, she watched her mother slowly disappear in the rearview mirror. She careened onto Creekside Drive with barely a glance in either direction. Tears blurring her vision, she smacked her palms against the steering wheel. "Ugh! I hate her!" The stoplight ahead turned red and she slammed on her brakes. She removed her cell phone from her bag and thumbed off a quick text to her new best friend: "*Heidi ambushed me at home. Why won't she won't leave me alone?*" She flung the phone onto the floor of the passenger's side.

When the light turned green, Annie took a sharp left onto Main Street instead of going straight toward Captain Sweeney's.

She punched the accelerator and sped through the business section of town, oblivious to the pedestrians milling about on the sidewalks and window-shopping despite the crisp February chill.

She was driving too fast to react when a Chrysler minivan veered over the line from oncoming traffic.

# TWO

## ELI

Lieutenant Eli Marshall usually left the responsibility of writing parking tickets to his rookie officers, but he couldn't let the owner of the red pickup truck with Texas license plates get away with parking in a designated handicap space without a permit. He was tucking the ticket beneath the windshield wiper when a car roared past on Main Street behind him. He looked up from his ticket, and then did a double take. *Annie?*

He hopped in his patrol car and pulled in behind Annie's Honda. He didn't want to have to give her a ticket. But Annie had gotten her license only a few months ago, and Mike had just given her the car for Christmas. A speeding ticket would be a lesson well learned if it saved her life one day.

He engaged his blue lights, preparing to pull her over, when the accident happened. Tires screeched and a horn blasted as the minivan swerved into Annie's lane. The sounds of metal crunching and glass shattering filled the air as her Honda hit the front end of the minivan, bounced off the curb, flipped over, and landed on its roof.

Eli shouted, "Oh my God almighty! Annie, no!" With shaking hands and racing heart, he maneuvered his cruiser through the wreckage to the side of the road and pulled in as close as he could to the overturned vehicle. He pressed the talk button on his headset and barked out orders to dispatch, summoning police backup as well as the fire and rescue departments. He jumped out of the cruiser and raced to Annie's side. The driver's window was broken, the shattered glass scattered all over the pavement. The air bag on the steering wheel had deployed, pinning Annie's body against the seat. She would surely have been ejected out of the car if she hadn't been wearing her seat belt. Blood gushed from a gash in her forehead and her left shoulder was cocked at an unnatural angle. He removed his bandanna from his pocket and pressed it to the wound, the blood quickly turning the blue-and-white fabric red.

"Annie, honey, it's Eli. Can you hear me?" When she didn't respond, his fingertips searched her neck for a pulse. He breathed a sigh of relief. "Hang in there, sweetheart. Help is on the way." As the sound of sirens grew louder, Eli whispered words of encouragement to Annie's unconscious body. He heard boots pounding the pavement and a hand grabbed him by the elbow. "We'll take it from here, Officer," said the owner of the boots, a beefy paramedic who appeared strong enough to lift the car with his pinky finger.

Straightening, Eli stepped away to allow the paramedics and firemen access to Annie. He surveyed the scene, searching for his backup who had yet to arrive. He saw the driver of the other vehicle, a woman in her midthirties, dazed and weeping beside the twisted wreckage of her minivan. Her entire front end was smashed, the engine hissing and a stream of green fluid running from beneath the car. Her air bag had also deployed, and as he approached her, he noticed minor lacerations on her neck and face. "Do you need medical attention?"

"I'm fine." She dropped her head and stared at the ground, her mouse-brown hair a curtain around her freckled face. She pointed a trembling finger at the other car. "Is she . . ." The woman gasped and her hand flew to her mouth. "Is she dead?"

"She has a pulse. That's all I know for now."

The woman whimpered and her body began to shake uncontrollably.

"Here." Eli removed his coat and draped it over her shoulders. The coat swallowed her petite frame. "Can you tell me what happened?"

"I was on my way to pick up my son from day care." Her hand gripping her cell phone, she gestured at the church building down the street.

"Miss, were you texting when the accident happened?"

Nodding, she bit down on her lip. "I was texting my husband. To tell him our son is sick."

"You may very well have cost the other driver her life. You realize that, don't you?"

Tears streamed down her cheeks. "I only took my eyes off the road for a second."

Eli sighed. "That's all it takes."

He was relieved to see the strobe of police lights arriving on the scene. In a matter of minutes, his reinforcements had taken control by setting off flairs and redirecting traffic. Luke Tanner, a rookie on the police force, strode toward them with a blanket in his hand. He removed Eli's jacket from the woman's shoulders and handed it to him. "What a mess. What happened?" he asked as he wrapped the blanket around the woman.

"Actually, I saw the whole thing. This woman veered across her lane into oncoming traffic." Eli pointed at the overturned vehicle. "The driver of that Honda over there didn't have time to stop."

"Because she was driving too fast!" the woman cried. "She could have killed me."

Luke removed his notepad from his top pocket. "Is that true?" he asked Eli.

*What good would it do to write Annie a ticket now? She's learning her lesson the hard way.* "She may have been driving a little over the limit, but let's not lose sight of the real issue. This woman was texting when the accident happened." Eli jabbed a finger at Luke's notepad. "Be sure to put that in your report. Can you take over for me here? I need to go check on Annie."

Luke's head shot up. "Annie? I hope you're not talking about Sam's Annie."

All eyes traveled to the overturned vehicle where the paramedics and firefighters were carefully extracting Annie's body from the wreckage.

Luke's mouth fell open. "Oh God! That is Annie." He gave Eli a gentle shove. "By all means, get over there."

As he hurried back to the overturned Honda, Eli clicked on his wife's number from his favorites list and pressed the phone to his ear. Sam answered on the fourth ring. "Where are you?"

"At Sweeney's. Waiting for Annie. I need to run some errands, but I can't leave until she gets here."

Eli drew in a deep breath. "I hate to be the one to tell you this, honey. But I have some bad news. Annie was involved in an accident a few minutes ago."

Sam gasped. "I heard the sirens. Is she okay?"

He craned his neck to peer over the paramedics gathered around Annie. They had placed her on a gurney and were preparing her for transport. She had an oxygen mask strapped to her face. "She's alive. That's all I know. Do you have any idea where Faith and Mike are?"

"Mike is already at the hospital, thank goodness. And Faith took Bitsy to a friend's house for a playdate. I'll call her now. Should we come there or meet you at the emergency room?"

The paramedics began to wheel Annie toward the ambulance. "Why don't you go straight to the hospital. I'll see you there."

He saw one of Annie's black Converse tennis shoes on the ground near her car. He scooped it up, stuffed it in his pocket, and stepped in line beside the paramedic with the muscles—Hank, according to his nametag. "How is she?"

Hank made a so-so gesture with his hand. "She's in and out of consciousness."

At five feet eight, Eli felt height challenged standing next to the beast. "May I speak to her? We're family."

Hank shot him a sideways glance. "Family how?"

"I'm her uncle. Her mother is my wife's sister."

Hank slowed the gurney to a stop at the back of the ambulance. "You can try, but she probably can't hear you."

"Hey, Annie baby, it's Eli. Can you hear me?" He wanted to touch her body, needed to feel the warmth of her skin for reassurance, but he was afraid he'd hurt her. She looked so pale and frail with her head braced between two supports and the bandage on her forehead already seeping with blood.

Annie's lids fluttered open and her brown eyes grew wide with fear.

He stroked her cheek to the right of the oxygen mask. "I know you're scared, honey. But you're gonna be okay. Mike's at the hospital. He'll take good care of you."

"Who is Mike?" Hank asked, as he prepared to lift the gurney into the ambulance.

"Her father, Mike Neilson. He's an ER doc."

"I know Mike. He's a good man." Hank climbed into the back of the ambulance behind the gurney.

"Will you radio him ahead and let him know you're coming?" Eli asked.

Hank offered him a thumbs-up as the rear doors slammed. Eli felt an ache in the back of his throat watching the ambulance speed off, lights flashing and siren blaring.

Eli wasn't Annie's uncle anymore than Mike was her father. He found his relationship with her difficult to explain. To the members of the Sweeney family, Annie was sister, cousin, niece, and daughter. But she was blood kin only to one. Jamie. Her half brother. His stepson. The boy Sam had raised on her own since his birth.

Eli thought back to the previous summer when he first met Annie. She'd shown up at Faith and Mike's wedding uninvited—filthy dirty and borderline malnourished, wearing threadbare clothes and dime-store flip-flops—in search of the half brother she'd never met. She needed Jamie's help in saving their father's life. Specifically, a section of his liver. But Allen had died before a decision could be made about a transplant operation, making Annie an orphan. At least that's what they'd thought at the time. Before Heidi had shown up out of the blue.

## THREE

Annie fought her way through the haze toward Eli's voice. She managed to open her eyes, but the mask covering her mouth prevented her from speaking. She couldn't tell exactly where it was coming from, but the pain was intolerable. She closed her eyes and retreated to the nothingness where everything was peaceful and nothing hurt.

The next time she came to, she rocketed through the fog like a spacecraft being launched into orbit. Her eyes bounced around the room, off the walls and ceiling and floor. She recognized the pale green walls, harsh overhead lighting, and stainless steel equipment of the emergency room. Mike's face came into view. She'd never been so happy to see his chubby rosy cheeks and twinkling blue eyes.

"Welcome back, sweetheart. You're in the emergency room at Prospect General. You took quite a blow to your head. Do you remember your name?"

Someone had replaced the oxygen mask with tubes in her nose. "Annie Bethune."

Mike directed a thumb at his chest. "Do you know who I am?"

The neck brace prevented her from nodding. "You're Mike Neilson, my legal guardian."

After Annie's father died, Faith and Mike had offered to adopt her, but the idea of a relationship so permanent terrified her no matter how kind they were. She'd grown to love them and knew them well, but her track record with parental units sucked. They'd agreed to become her legal guardians instead.

Mike flashed a penlight in her eyes. "Can you tell me where it hurts?"

"Everywhere."

He chuckled. "In your case, that's actually a good sign." He squeezed her right hand. "Can you feel this?"

"Yes."

He pinched the tip of her index finger on her left hand. "And this."

"Uh-huh."

"How about this?" He ran a cold metal object up the bottoms of both her feet.

"Yes, I can feel that. Does this mean we can take off this neck brace? It's choking me."

He smiled. "Not quite yet, but soon."

Tears spilled over her lids and ran down her cheeks. "I'm so sorry, Mike. I didn't mean to wreck the car. The van came outta nowhere. She was in front of me and I couldn't stop."

He snatched a tissue from the box on the counter behind him. "That's what insurance is for, honey." He mopped up her tears. "My only concern right now is your health. I'm gonna fix you up good as new, but you'll need to cooperate. It won't be easy."

"I can't stand the pain, Mike. My left arm feels like a shark ripped it off. And my head is killing me, like someone chopped it open with an ax."

"I'll give you something for the pain in a minute. But I'm not going to lie to you, Annie. You're pretty banged up. We'll have to take some X-rays. We may even need to do an MRI." He turned his back on her for a moment as he consulted his clipboard, and then turned back to face her. "I'm required to ask this of all my female patients of childbearing age. Is there any chance you could be pregnant?"

She stared at him, waiting for him to smile and say, "April Fool's," like he always did even though it wasn't April 1. When his face remained impassive, she averted her eyes. Was it possible she was pregnant? She'd missed her period, but that was nothing new. She wasn't exactly regular.

Her mind drifted back six weeks to New Year's Eve.

She'd been dating Cooper since Thanksgiving at his family's farm when they'd finally admitted their attraction to one another was more than friendship. Neither of them had ever been in a serious relationship. And they were both virgins. They'd agreed to take the sex part slow, but in an intense moment on New Year's Eve, they let things go too far. His parents were out of town. Snuggled up on the floor in front of the gas fire, they drank a glass of champagne to toast in the New Year while watching *Dick Clark's New Year's Rockin' Eve*. Innocent kisses led to heavy petting. She had squirmed and he had fumbled and groped. The whole awkward encounter hadn't lasted long. She'd experienced no pain and there'd been no blood. Naturally she'd assumed he hadn't popped her cherry.

After the clock stroked midnight, while he was driving her home, Cooper asked, "You don't think you could have gotten . . . I mean, we didn't use any protection."

She waved him off. "I'm sure it's fine." She rested her head against his chest. "Technically speaking, I'm not even sure we did it." She used air quotes to emphasize the *it*. "It didn't hurt like everyone says it does. But it didn't feel good either. I don't get all the hype."

"Next time will be better." He kissed her hair. "I don't think either one of us was ready for it tonight. It's my fault for letting things get out of control."

"I don't think the next time should be anytime soon." She smiled to herself at their innocence. "We're probably the only teenage couple in America who isn't having sex every chance we get."

Cooper scrunched up his brow. "If that's supposed to make me feel better, it doesn't."

She nudged him. "Don't be so sensitive. I didn't mean to offend you. I'm laughing because we're so naive."

"No, you're right. Clearly, I'm the one with the problem," Cooper said under his breath. And he'd barely spoken to her since.

"Annie, sweetheart, can you hear me?" Mike's lips were close to her ear. When she didn't respond, he snapped his fingers in front of her face. "Come on, Annie. I need for you to pay attention, so we can move forward with your treatment."

She locked eyes with his.

"It's in the best interest of your health for you to tell me the truth. Is there any chance you're pregnant? You can trust me. You should know that by now."

"Yes," she mumbled. "But please don't tell Faith."

## FOUR

Sam beat Eli to the hospital. She was sitting alone in a long line of empty chairs when he arrived. An elderly man with a bloody kitchen towel draped over his hand and a teenage mother cradling a sleeping infant in her arms were the only other people in the ER waiting room.

"Come here, you." He pulled Sam from her chair and held her at arm's length, taking her in from the top of her cropped blonde head to her dark-washed jeans and the pointy toes of her cowboy boots, relieved to see she hadn't changed since breakfast. Sensing the worry behind her deep blue eyes, he wrapped his arms around her slight frame and buried his face in the soft spot at the crook of her neck. "You never know when you wake up in the morning what the day will bring."

Sam ran her hands up and down his back. "You're shaking all over. Are you okay?"

He choked back a sob. "Not really, no. The accident happened right in front of me. I was powerless to do anything to stop it. I can't even think about what might have happened if she hadn't been wearing her seat belt."

"Let's sit down." Sam lowered herself to her chair and pulled him down beside her. "Take deep breaths. Try to clear your mind."

"I saw her car flip over with my own eyes, Sammie. I'm not sure I'll ever be able to erase that image from my mind." Eli propped his elbow on the arm of the chair and buried his face in his hand. "We should probably call Jamie."

"I already thought about that. Let's wait until we know more about Annie's condition. Jamie has a lot of work this week. Knowing him, he'll want to jump in the car and drive down here. Same goes for Mom. She finally seems to be dealing with Mack's death and now this. She loves Annie. I'd hate to think of what she'd do if something happens to her." Sam slipped her arm through his, resting her head against him. They stayed that way until Faith charged through the plate glass doors ten minutes later. Sam and Eli stood and greeted her with hugs.

Faith's brown hair was tied back in a haphazard ponytail and the lines around her hazel eyes were etched with concern. "I'm sorry it took me so long. I had to go by the house and feed the puppy. Have you heard anything?"

"Not yet," Sam said. "An ambulance arrived a few minutes ago. I imagine that was Annie. But I haven't seen or heard from Mike."

Faith held up the phone she gripped tightly in her hand. "I just texted him to let him know I was here."

Faith slipped off her fleece and they all sat down.

"Where's Bitsy?" Sam asked.

"I left her with the Cooks. Kathy, the mother, offered to keep Bitsy overnight and take her to school in the morning." She leaned over Sam and said, "Eli, how much do you know about the accident?"

Eli inhaled a deep breath. "I was there at the time. I was writing a parking ticket on Main Street, in front of The Grill, when Annie sped past me."

Faith scrunched up her brow. "Speeding? Are you sure? That

doesn't sound like Annie. She drives like a granny. I should know. I'm the one who taught her."

"Surprised me, too, honestly," Eli said. "But she was definitely driving too fast for that portion of Main Street. Maybe she wasn't aware that the speed limit is only thirty-five through there. Or maybe she wasn't paying attention. I followed her, planning to pull her over and give her a warning. Just to scare her, you understand. But then a car coming from the opposite direction veered across the line. The woman admitted to texting at the time."

"Do you have any idea where Annie was headed?" Sam asked. "Why would she have been going east on Main Street, away from the market, when she was already late to work?"

"I have no idea, but wherever she was going, she was in a hurry to get there."

"I talked to her as she was leaving the parking lot at school," Faith said. "She was going to stop by the house to change and go straight to work."

"Something must've happened," Sam said. "Maybe she and Cooper got in a fight or something."

Faith asked, "Did you get a chance to talk to her, Eli?"

"She was in and out of consciousness," Eli said. "I spoke to her as the paramedics were wheeling her to the ambulance. She opened her eyes, and I think she recognized me, but the oxygen mask prevented her from responding."

Tears filled Faith's eyes and she brought a trembling fist to her mouth. "Sounds like her injuries are serious."

Eli nodded. "I hate to alarm you, Faith, but you need to be prepared for some bad news. Her car overturned. She's lucky to be alive."

"But she's in the best hands, honey," Sam said, rubbing her sister's thigh. "Mike will take good care of her."

"I know," Faith said, drawing in an unsteady breath and swiping at her tears.

In the back corner of the waiting room, a television caught

their attention with its early edition of the local news. The lead story featured the accident on Main Street, which continued to create havoc for afternoon commuters. The reporter broadcasted the details. A young mother, texting at the time, swerved into oncoming traffic. A teenage girl seriously injured. Authorities still working to clear the scene.

Faith twisted in her seat to see the TV.

"I wouldn't look if I were you," Eli said. "Believe me when I tell you that you don't want that image in your mind."

"Good point," Faith said, and turned back around.

The threesome waited in silence. They crossed and uncrossed their legs, twiddled their thumbs, watched the minutes tick by on the wall clock opposite them, and fiddled with their phones. But their eyes never left the double doors leading to the examining rooms.

A stunning young black girl with a flawless complexion, pert nose, and amber eyes—about sixteen years old if Eli had to guess —entered the ER just as the early edition of the news was ending. Three pairs of eyes followed her across the room to the reception desk where she inquired about Annie Bethune.

The threesome sat up straighter in their chairs, straining to hear the conversation.

The disinterested nurse, an older woman with hair more violet than silver, at the reception desk asked, "Are you family?"

"No. But I'm a friend." The girl cast a nervous glance around the waiting room.

"I'm sorry, but we're not allowed to release patient information to *friends*." The nurse's lip curled up as if she found the word distasteful. "I suggest you come back in the morning."

When the girl turned to leave, Eli rose from his chair and stepped in her path. Sam and Faith joined him. "I couldn't help but overhear you inquiring about Annie," he said. "We're her family."

Her golden eyes sought out his nametag. "Oh right. You're

Eli. I've heard a lot about you." She looked first at his wife and then her sister. "You must be Sam and Faith."

Eli wondered how she knew so much about them when they knew nothing about her. "And you are?"

"Althea Bell. But everyone calls me Thea. I'm a friend of Annie's."

His eyebrows shot up. "Did you say Bell? Are you any kin to Flora?"

Coils of hair danced around Thea's face as she nodded her head. "I'm her daughter. How do you know my mama?"

"I used to eat breakfast with her at The Grill at least three times a week. She sure could pour a mean cup of coffee. I've missed old Flora. How's she feeling?"

A pained expression crossed her face. "She has good days and bad days. The doctor's after her to lose some weight, but so far, none of the diets have done any good. She's still smiling, though. You know Mama."

"I know that smile well." The image of Flora's bright face lifted his spirits. "What about your brothers? Are they still giving her a hard time?"

Thea shuffled her feet. "Pretty much, yeah. They have good days and bad days too. They help us out a lot with the bills." She stared down at the ground. "If only they'd come up with a better way to earn their money."

Eli raised an eyebrow. "How do they make their money now, Thea?"

"I suspect you already know the answer to that." She brightened. "I'm working at The Grill now." She held open her down jacket to reveal a red apron she wore over black pants and a white polo. "I was serving a table by the window when the accident happened. I saw the whole thing. But I didn't get Annie's text until ten minutes ago when I went on break."

Thea removed her phone from the apron pocket and handed it to Eli. He read the text out loud. "*Heidi ambushed me at home.*

*Why won't she leave me alone?"* He slid the text bubble to the side to show the time. "She texted this at eleven minutes past four." He removed his ticket book from his jacket pocket. "I was writing a ticket for the owner of a pickup parked in a handicapped spot across from The Grill just prior to the accident. I documented that time as 4:13 p.m."

Faith massaged her temples. "Annie knows better than to text while driving."

"Let's not jump to conclusions," Sam said. "For all we know, the light was red and Annie was stopped when she texted this. What's more important is her frame of mind at the time. Sounds like she was upset about Heidi's visit."

"Which might explain why she was speeding," Eli said.

Thea gestured at the reception desk. "That old lady won't tell me anything. Is Annie gonna be okay?"

"We don't know anything yet either. We're still waiting to hear from the doctor." Sam pulled her phone out of her bag. "If you'll give me your number, I'll text you as soon as we do."

Thea recited the number. "I need to get back to work," she said, with a glance toward the exit. "My ride is waiting for me outside."

Eli, Sam, and Faith walked Thea to the door and stood watching as she drove off in a low-slung compact car with tinted windows and black rims. They were headed back to their seats when the double doors opened and Mike emerged from the treatment area, dressed in scrubs with his stethoscope draped over his neck. His slumped posture and solemn expression warned Eli to prepare for the worst.

## FIVE

## HEIDI

Hugh held the door open for Heidi, welcoming her into her own apartment upon her return from Prospect. Her neck prickled, an army of ants crawling across her skin. Did being her landlord allow him unrestricted access to her home without her permission?

"How'd you get in?" she asked.

"I have a spare key." He held up a silver door key. "Just in case of emergencies." He pinched her chin in response to her concerned look. "Don't worry. I promise not to abuse my land-lord privileges."

What *privileges did* he have as her landlord? She'd never thought to ask.

Heidi had first met Hugh six weeks ago when she'd signed the lease on the apartment, the whole second floor of the federal-style single house he'd recently renovated on Broad Street. She'd moved in on December twenty-eighth. Then, three days later, they'd bumped into one another, both alone, at a bar on New Year's Eve. They'd seen each other nearly every day since.

She brushed past him, and dropped her bag onto a nearby bench.

"I didn't mean to upset you." He held the key out in the palm of his hand. "Please, take the key if it makes you uncomfortable. I would never enter your home without your permission to fix a leaky pipe under the sink. But I knew how important today was for you. I didn't want you coming home to an empty house."

She turned to him, staring into his warm chocolate eyes. *What are you thinking, Heidi?* She mentally chastised herself. Having this sexy man—with his salt-and-pepper hair and easy smile, wearing his faded jeans and workman's boots—greet her upon her return was the best thing that had happened to her all day. Although the jury was still out—she needed a little more time to deliberate, another month to be certain that this lovely man was for real, that a Dr. Hyde personality wasn't waiting in the wings for the right moment to reveal itself—it was possible that he was the best thing that had happened to her in her whole life. Aside from Annie.

She folded his fingers around the key. "Keep it." She took his scruffy face in her hands and kissed him hard on the lips. "You can welcome me home anytime."

"If you greet me like this, I will." He kissed her back with more urgency. "I'd love to sweep you off your feet and carry you into the bedroom right now. But first, I want to hear about your meeting with Annie."

She drew away from him. "It didn't go well." Her voice quivered and she willed herself not to cry.

"I was afraid of that. Come with me." He took her by the hand and led her across the room to the fireplace, where the flames from the gas logs flickered. He'd set a tray with two espressos and a plate of her favorite almond chocolate biscotti biscuits on the coffee table in front of her turquoise sofa.

"Sit down and tell me everything." They sat down side by side on the sofa, the closeness of his body offering her comfort.

"There's not much to tell actually. Annie flat out refuses to talk to me. She and I were getting along so well when I was Heidi the Caterer planning Sam's wedding. I wish we could go back to the way things were before."

***

She sipped her espresso while she thought back to December when she'd first *met* Annie. Relatively speaking of course, considering she'd known her for a brief time as a baby. Heidi had done her homework when she moved to Charleston last August. She'd hired a private investigator who'd discovered that Annie's father, Allen, had died from liver cancer, and Annie was living with the Sweeney family in Prospect. Networking her way from one family member to the next, she managed to land a job catering Sam Sweeney's wedding reception, a small sit-down luncheon for family and a few friends on Christmas Eve. Heidi used the opportunity to get close to her daughter. She never dreamed she'd end up working with her side by side planning the reception. Much to Heidi's delight, she and Annie had gotten along swimmingly from the start. They had a lot in common, and not just about food. They talked for hours about everything and nothing. She'd planned to wait until things settled down after the holidays to reveal her true identity to Annie. Truth be told, she was terrified of breaking the news for obvious reasons. But that bit of unpleasantness took care of itself.

They woke on Christmas Eve to snowfall, a rare phenomenon for the Lowcountry. The snow added to the already-festive mood, and the wedding luncheon went off without a hitch. Annie was helping Heidi clean up afterward when that mood soured. On her way from the dining room with a stack of dirty plates, Annie collided with one of the chairs at the kitchen table, sending Heidi's handbag tumbling to the floor.

"Oh my gosh," Annie said, staring down at the pocketbook's paraphernalia spilled out across the hardwood. "I'm so sorry."

"No worries. I'll get it." Heidi was elbow-deep in soapy water. Before she could dry her hands, Annie had set the stack of plates on the counter and bent down to gather up the contents of her bag.

"What's this?" Annie asked, holding up Heidi's California driver's license. Heidi hadn't taken the time to get a new one since moving to South Carolina. "Says here that your name is Sandra Bethune. I don't understand. I thought your name was Heidi Butler."

"Heidi is my stage name. I was once an actress. Not a very good one obviously, since I'm catering wedding luncheons instead of starring in movies," she said, trying to make light of the situation while hoping Annie wouldn't connect the dots.

"My last name is Bethune," Annie said, her voice no more than a whisper. "And my real mother's name is Sandra. Are you . . .?"

Heidi could still remember the hurt on Annie's face when she realized she'd been betrayed.

---

"Try not to worry about it, sweetheart." Hugh massaged Heidi's neck, his contractor's hands callused and rough against her skin. "Annie is a confused teenager whose biological mother has suddenly reappeared in her life after sixteen years. She needs time to adjust."

Heidi rubbed her tired eyes, smearing her mascara in the process. "If only she'd give me a chance to explain, I think I could get her to understand why I made the choices I did."

He pulled her close. "You've told me very little about that time in your life. You can talk to me. I won't judge you. I promise."

Heidi and Hugh had talked about everything. He knew she

wore a neon-pink shade of lipstick called Candy Yum-Yum, and she knew he ate ketchup on his grits and snored when he drank whiskey. But neither of them had shared too much about their pasts. What scared her most about her relationship with Hugh was that he would dump her once he discovered the truth.

But she couldn't keep it from him forever.

She drew in an unsteady breath. "I'm so ashamed of the way I behaved back then. I can justify abandoning my six-month-old daughter by blaming it on my age and lack of maturity. All the other bad decisions are what keep me awake at night. It only took a couple of years for me to figure out I wasn't going to be the next Reese Witherspoon. I should have come home to my family then. I never sent her a single birthday card or Christmas present. I've never once tried to call her, or my husband for that matter, in all these years. We were still married when he died."

"I'm confused. Why didn't you get in touch with them?" Despite his promise not to judge her, Heidi detected criticism in his voice.

"Pride. It was easier to hide out in California, pretending all those glamorous movie stars were my friends. Sad thing is, I was never good enough to be anything but their cook. Some mark I made on Hollywood."

"Here. Eat this." He held a biscotti biscuit in front of her nose. "Chocolate always makes you feel better." She smiled and crunched off a bite. He placed the rest of the biscuit on a napkin and handed it to her. "You're a good person who lost her way. It happens to the best of us. You'll have to work hard, but you'll get back on the right path."

Heidi shook her head, her messy bun flopping around on top. "I'm not sure I can handle the rejection."

"Sure you can." Hugh tucked a loose strand of hair behind her ear. "You know what you want. You just need to figure out how to get it."

"What if she never forgives me?"

"Then she never forgives you. But you can't give up without trying."

"I don't know, Hugh. I was so hopeful about today. I've daydreamed about our reconciliation a thousand times." A smile spread across Heidi's lips as she imagined it. "Me offering my heartfelt apology, and her forgiving me for leaving. Me inviting her to come live here, and her jumping at the opportunity for us to be together as mother and daughter—or as friends. I'll take either." She set her biscuit down on the table. "It was nothing but a foolish fantasy. I see that now."

"Nothing about your dream is foolish. Being reunited with your daughter is your end goal. But you can't just waltz into town and demand to be a part of Annie's life. Right now she doesn't care what prompted you to run off to Hollywood. All she knows is that you abandoned her as a baby. Back off and give her some space. Let her come to you. When she does, be a good listener. Let her talk about *her* feelings. But you'd better prepare yourself, because what she says may not be easy for you to hear. This is about her. This is not about you."

Tears stung Heidi's clear green eyes. "Are you calling me self-centered?" She looked away from him. "Never mind. Don't answer that. I know it's true." Annie had accused her of that very thing. *Because you never bothered to find out.* "I stink at relationships. I'm better off moving to Alaska and living the life of an Eskimo."

"Look who's feeling sorry for herself," Hugh said, running his finger down her cheek. "Please don't move to Alaska. I'd be sad to see you go. I haven't been this happy in twenty years."

"We've only been dating six weeks, Hugh. I don't usually screw things up with a man before the two-month mark," she said, settling back against the soft velvet cushions. "Okay, so now that I've told you all my darkest secrets, it's your turn to talk about that thing you never talk about."

"What thing is that?"

She kicked off her booties and tucked her legs up beneath her. "That invisible elephant in the room. If I knew what it was, I wouldn't have to ask. But I know you're hiding something, Hugh Kelley."

"All right. I guess it's time I tell you about my wife." He shifted away from her, facing forward, staring into the fire. "In the beginning, I was so head over heels in love with April, and naive to human nature, to recognize her neediness as narcissism. We were well into our second year of marriage when I realized I was the only one in the relationship doing any giving. Her fertility problems only made matters worse. When none of the procedures worked, she sunk into deep depression. She stopped working. Stopped seeing friends. Refused to consider adoption or seek therapy for her depression. Out of desperation, in an attempt to save our marriage, I started seeing a counselor. But nothing I tried, and I tried everything, improved our relationship. After she died, I needed more therapy to deal with the guilt."

Heidi ran her finger across the dark stubble on his cheek. "Why should you feel guilty when you did everything you could to try and help her?"

He got up and went to the window, peeling back the sheer curtain. "My wife didn't die in a car accident like I led you to believe. April took her own life."

Heidi experienced a sinking feeling in her gut, like she'd swallowed a bowling ball. She left the sofa and went to him. "I'm so sorry, Hugh. That must have been awful for you."

Hugh nodded. "It was a difficult time, but I didn't mean to make this conversation about me."

"I asked, remember?" She hooked her arm around his neck and pulled his lips to hers. "Now we don't have any secrets from one another."

The distant ringing of her phone interrupted their kiss. She pushed away from him and retrieved the phone from her bag.

Her stomach lurched when she saw Sam Sweeney's name on the screen.

She punched the green button and accepted the call. "Sam? Is everything okay?"

"I'm afraid not. Annie has been in an accident."

## SIX

ANNIE

Annie drifted in and out of her drug-induced sleep. Bit by bit she became aware of her surroundings. The television mounted on the wall opposite her. Daylight streaming through the metal blinds in the window to her right. The IV stand dripping liquids through a clear tube to the needle in her arm. The beep of the heart monitor somewhere behind her head. Thea, stretched out in the recliner in the corner, staring at her phone. She was wearing Annie's favorite outfit—a red turtleneck sweater and pleated plaid skirt, her brown legs showing above her taupe suede boots. Her friend's wardrobe was limited, but the clothes she owned, she wore with style.

Annie tried to sit up. "Where am I?"

Thea brought her chair upright and walked the short distance to the bed. "You're in the hospital. Do you remember what happened?"

Annie winced at the pain in her head. She recalled bits and pieces. The van cutting in front of her. She was driving too fast to stop. The terrified expression on the other driver's face. Being in the emergency room with Mike. There was something important she was supposed to remember about that—about her encounter with Mike in the emergency room—dancing on the periphery of her mind, taunting her to remember but escaping her when she tried.

"Where's Mike?" she murmured. Her throat was so dry, her lips parched.

Thea shrugged. "I haven't seen anyone since I got here twenty minutes ago."

She licked her lips. "No one? Not Faith or Sam?"

"Nope. They were here last night with Eli when I stopped by the emergency room during my break."

She searched the walls for a clock. Seven thirty. "I guess it's still early. How did you know? About the accident, I mean."

"I was working at the time, waiting on a table over by the window. I saw the accident happen."

Annie felt like she was floating in a warm bathtub. She watched the blanket as she wiggled her toes. She lifted her right arm, but the tape from the IV pinched, and she lay it back down. She couldn't move her left arm at all. "I feel numb all over. How bad are my injuries?"

"I don't know. They were still waiting to hear from the doctors when I was here last night. Sam texted me around eleven to tell me you were okay and that they were admitting you, but she didn't say anything about how bad you were hurt. You got a big bandage on your forehead, near your temple. Other than that, you look pretty good to me for someone whose car turned over at forty-five miles an hour."

Annie experienced a sudden flash of memory—of her being pinned against the seat by the air bag and the searing pain in her neck and shoulder. "I remember some of that. I can't believe my car turned over. Was I really driving that fast?"

Thea sat down gingerly on the edge of the mattress. "I can't say for sure how fast you were driving, but you were going at a pretty good clip when you passed by The Grill. The speed limit is only thirty-five on that section of Main Street. You usually drive slower than my mama. Did something happen with Heidi that got you so worked up?"

The confrontation with Heidi rushed back to Annie like a hot gust of wind on a still summer day. "Yes! And it's all her fault. We got in a big fight."

"You texted me about that, right before the accident happened." Thea located the text on her phone and showed it to Annie: "*Heidi ambushed me at home. Why won't she leave me alone?*"

"I remember. I was at the stoplight. When the light turned green, instead of going straight to the market, I took a left onto Main Street. I was crying. I didn't want Sam to see me upset."

"What did Heidi say that made you so upset?"

"More of the same of her sorry excuses and pleas for forgiveness. She's a broken record." Imitating a sickly sweet voice, Annie said, "*I'm so sorry. Please forgive me. Give me a chance to explain.* Blah, blah, blah. How can she expect me to just forget that she abandoned me as a baby? I have a good life now with Faith and Mike. What if she screws that up for me?"

"You'll be seventeen in May. One more year and you're free to do anything you want."

"Ha. Those fifteen months feel like an eternity to me." She licked her lips again. "Could you get me some water, please?"

Thea retrieved a Styrofoam cup of ice chips from the rolling bed table. "Here." She spooned some chips onto Annie's tongue.

"Aren't you gonna be late for school?" Annie asked, crunching the ice with her teeth.

"I'll leave in a minute. Mrs. Robinson won't mind if I'm late for homeroom." Thea continued to feed Annie small spoonfuls of chips. "Do you think anyone called Cooper?"

"Why would anyone call Cooper? I don't want him here." No sooner had she spoken than that important thing Annie was supposed to remember about Mike and the ER popped into her head, gripping her chest and taking her breath away. She pushed Thea's hand away. "That's enough. Thanks."

Thea found the remote and clicked on the morning news. "I heard someone in the lobby say it might snow this weekend. I'd be down with not having school on Monday."

While the meteorologist discussed the possibility of winter precipitation, Annie thought back to the last time it had snowed in Prospect. During Sam's wedding on Christmas Eve. When everything had still been right in her world. The same day she discovered that Heidi was her mother. One week before her relationship with Cooper had taken a sharp turn south on New Year's Eve.

She rolled her head toward Thea. "Do you remember what I told you about New Year's Eve, about what happened between Cooper and me out at the farm?"

Thea shifted her attention from the weather forecast back to Annie. "Of course I remember. I never forget the sex parts."

Annie's lips hurt when she smiled. "I don't know as much about these things as you. But remember I told you how awkward the sex had been, and that I wasn't even sure we'd done it right."

Thea nodded. "Go on."

"Do you think there's any chance I could have gotten pregnant?"

"Girl!" Thea said, her amber eyes widening. "Please tell me you used protection."

Tears welled up in her eyes. "We weren't planning on having sex that night."

Thea clicked the weeks off on her fingers. "That was almost six weeks ago. Did you skip your monthly?"

"I guess. I'd forgotten all about it until last night when Mike asked me if there was any chance I might be pregnant. They always ask you that before they do X-rays."

"What did you tell him?"

A tear rolled down her cheek. "I told him the truth. And I asked him not to tell Faith."

"Tell me what?" Faith asked from the doorway. She entered the room, and set a duffel bag on the bed at Annie's feet. "If you're talking about your run-in with Heidi yesterday, I already know about it." She dipped her head at Thea. "It's nice to see you again so soon."

When Faith bent over to kiss Annie's cheek, Thea crossed her eyes and swiped at her forehead in relief.

"You went through quite an ordeal yesterday. How do you feel?" Faith pressed the back of her hand to Annie's forehead as though checking for fever.

"Numb. Like I'm floating on a life raft in the middle of the ocean."

"That's the morphine," Faith said. "You're pretty banged up."

"Can you be a little more specific? I can wiggle most of my fingers and toes. Except the ones on my left hand. I guess that means I'm not paralyzed. What's wrong with my arm?"

"It's not your arm," Faith said. "The problem is with your shoulder. The doctors aren't certain about the extent of the damage. They're gonna do an MRI this morning to determine whether you need surgery. Aside from that, you have a couple of broken ribs, a two-inch laceration on your forehead, and a concussion to go along with it. The plastic surgeon who sewed you up has assured us you won't have a scar."

Annie was almost afraid to ask, "Anything else?"

Thea laughed. "Isn't that enough?"

"There's always a risk for internal bleeding," Faith explained. "But that's looking less and less likely with each passing hour."

*Phew!* Annie thought. Maybe the pregnancy test came back negative. Or maybe she'd imagined the whole exchange with Mike in the ER. She was on heavy-duty painkillers after all. Or maybe he'd honored her wishes and hadn't broken the news to

Faith yet. Which meant she might still be pregnant. "Where's Mike?"

"He wanted to stay with you, but I insisted he go home after his shift and get some sleep."

"Did you stay here all night?"

Faith smiled. "Of course. I wasn't about to leave you alone. I went home for a few minutes earlier to get some of your things."

"What about Bitsy? Don't you need to take her to school?"

"She spent the night with a friend. She doesn't know about the accident yet." Faith turned her attention to Thea, who had been inching her way toward the door. "Speaking of school, aren't you going to be late?"

"Probably. I should get going." Thea tugged on Annie's big toe through the blanket. "I'll text you later."

"Wait a minute." Annie's eyes traveled the room. "Where's my phone and my purse? Did anyone get my stuff out of the car?"

"Hmm. That's a good question." Faith opened the door to the wardrobe. "They aren't in here. I don't remember anyone saying anything about your belongings last night. I'll get Mike and Eli to check on them for you."

"I'm off, then," Thea said, with a half wave. "Since you don't have your phone, I'll stop by after school on my way to work."

Faith crossed the room to the doorway and stuck her head out into the hallway for several seconds. She turned back around, pulling the door closed behind her. "Annie, honey, there's something I need to talk to you about."

Annie braced herself. *Here it comes.*

## SEVEN

## COOPER

Cooper dragged himself out of bed after the third snooze cycle and lumbered down the hall to the bathroom. He splashed cold water on his face, then raked his fingers through his unruly copper mop, brushed his teeth, and ran his electric razor over his cheeks. Returning to his room, he dressed in jeans and a gray flannel shirt. He gathered his books and computer from his desk, and stuffed them into his backpack. He slashed through the block for yesterday's date, February eighth, on his Duck's Unlimited calendar. Six months, give or take a few days, before he left for college. *If* he could ever decide on a college. There were so many factors to consider. Disappointing his parents. Being separated from his twin brother. Getting as far away from Annie as possible.

He found his mother in the kitchen serving up pancakes with a spatula. Her dark hair was pulled back on her neck, and despite the early hour, her lips were painted the color of ripe plums. Cooper wondered if his friends' mothers put on lipstick before they brushed their teeth in the morning.

"When did you get home?" he asked. His mother spent much

of the week in Charleston where her interior design firm, JSH Designs, was based. The JSH stood for Jacqueline Sweeney Hart, his uber-sophisticated mother who had always been somewhat of an enigma to him. She reminded him of the fragile model boat that sat on the shelf in their living room, the family's cherished possession that he and his brother were allowed to look at but never to touch. Cooper's grandmother, Lovie Sweeney, had commissioned a professional to replicate the commercial fishing boat his grandfather, Oscar, had fished from every day of his life until his passing nearly seven years ago. His mother and her sisters, Sam and Faith, had drawn straws to determine who would keep the model of the *My Three Gulls*, named after Oscar's three daughters.

"Late last night, after you'd gone to bed." She placed a plate in front of him. "I just received some disturbing news." She slid onto the chair next to him. "Aunt Sam called. Did you know Annie was in a car accident yesterday afternoon after school?"

"Yeah. Some of my friends were texting me about that. I had to turn my phone off so I could finish my art project." Cooper forked off a bite of sausage and stuffed it in his mouth. "She's okay, right?"

Jackie folded her arms on the table and leaned in closer to him. "Her car overturned on Main Street, Cooper. She's lucky to be alive. She has a concussion, a significant laceration on her head, a couple of broken ribs, and a crushed shoulder that will likely require surgery."

"That doesn't sound good," he mumbled. He couldn't bear to think of Annie in pain. It hurt too much to think of her at all these days. He reached for the syrup. Eating would help take his mind off the whole situation, at least for a little while.

"I'm surprised you're not camped out at the hospital. Did the two of you break up?"

"Not officially, no."

Jackie placed her hand on his arm, preventing him from taking another bite. "I'm warning you, son. I'm quite fond of that girl. Don't you dare hurt her."

"Geez, Mom. I'm fond of her too. Obviously." That was the problem. His feelings for Annie scared the hell out of him.

She released his arm. "I hope you mean that. Because, considering the dynamics of this family, an ugly breakup between the two of you could cause friction."

He hung his head. "I'm aware."

His mother got up and returned to the stove, ladling out another batch of pancakes for his brother. Sean made them late for school nearly every morning. Most days, Cooper was tempted to leave him, to teach him a lesson. But as he well knew, his brother would march straight back upstairs, crawl in bed, and hide out in his room for the rest of the day. He couldn't do that to his brother. He wouldn't let Sean get in trouble for skipping school. Instead, he let Sean's bad habits control his life. When they were little, maybe eight or nine years old, they'd discovered a giant clam while on vacation in the Caribbean. They had broken the clam in two and each boy had taken one of the shells, stashing it amongst their treasures as representation of their unique bond. Cooper didn't want to be a half anymore. He wanted to be whole.

He set his fork down on his plate, the untouched chunk of sausage stuck to the tines. His appetite had vanished, not that he'd had much of one in recent weeks. His life was so screwed up. But as much as he wanted to rush over to the hospital and see for himself that Annie was okay, he knew his sudden reappearance in her life would only make matters worse. He thought about how he had ignored her for the past month, and about the hurt he'd observed on her face when he passed her in the hallway at school without stopping to speak. He couldn't very well show up at her bedside and say, "Sorry, I've been an ass, but everything's okay now," when it wasn't.

He pushed back from the table and walked his plate to the sink. He scraped the remainder of his breakfast down the disposal and placed the plate in the dishwasher. Returning to the breakfast room, he hoisted his backpack over his shoulder and said to his mother without so much as a glance in her direction, "Tell Sean I'm waiting for him in the car."

Cooper inserted the key in the ignition and prayed the engine would start. He and Sean had saved their money from working summers at their family's seafood market to buy the 1991 Land Cruiser. They regretted that decision nearly everyday. The Cruiser had swag. No doubt about it. But something was always broken. This week the heat wouldn't work. He dialed the thermostat up on the off chance hot air might circulate through the vents. His father had talked about buying them a new car, something reliable, to take to college. One more thing they would share. One more thing that bound him to his twin.

Cooper's mother had been disappointed when he'd declined his early decision offer to attend her alma mater, the University of Georgia. A big southern SEC school was a better fit for Sean, who was all about fraternities and football. Contrary to his brother, Cooper was more interested in his academics. His passion for graphic design was a recent discovery. He was just beginning to explore his many options. He hadn't decided whether he wanted to go into design, marketing, or web development. His top choices for schools were in Savannah, Richmond, and New York. Only a two-hour drive from Prospect, Savannah was too close to home. Too close to Annie. While the best jobs in marketing and advertisement were located in Manhattan, a boy from a small inlet town in South Carolina would be fish bait for the big players in a large northern city. VCU seemed like the perfect solution. Richmond, similar to Charleston in its history and traditions, was far enough from home without requiring travel by plane.

He'd applied to all three schools, but he wouldn't hear from any of them until March. The waiting was torture.

Cooper blasted the horn, settled back in his seat, and wrapped his coat tighter around him. He had no clue what to do about Annie. He'd fallen head over heels for her the first time he set eyes on her at his Aunt Faith's wedding last June. She was the kind of girl he always imagined he'd marry. Wholesome. Resourceful. Compassionate. But his hopes and dreams for the future had changed. He no longer wanted to be a doctor like his father. And Prospect suddenly felt confining. Although he would miss the outdoors. He'd always imagined teaching his children to hunt and fish and love the water like his father and grandfather had taught him. Maybe he was going through some kind of phase. Maybe his newfound obsession with digital illustrations wasn't the pathway to a successful future. His art and photography teachers claimed he had potential. The techniques he'd learned from them had made his work stronger. But his true talent had yet to be tested.

The back door banged open and Sean hurried around to the passenger side. He dropped his backpack on the floorboard and buckled his seat belt. "Dude. When did it get so cold?" Sean said, blowing into his cupped hands.

"It's February. What do you expect?" Cooper said as he put the car in reverse. "Thanks to you, I'm going to be late to art again."

Sean play-punched him in the arm. "Lighten up, man. We're on senior slide. Our grades this semester don't matter."

"They matter to me." Cooper turned the Land Cruiser around and took off down the winding tree-lined driveway.

"What's with the bad mood, bro?" Sean snapped his fingers. "Oh, that's right. I heard about Annie. How does one roll a car on Main Street? The speed limit's like thirty-five through there. Unless, of course, she was speeding. One of my friends who saw her said she was flying down the road. Do you think she was speeding? She wasn't seriously hurt or anything, was she? Have you talked to her? I guess not, since y'all are broken up. Y'all *are* broken up, aren't you? I haven't seen you together in like a month."

Cooper couldn't help but laugh at his brother's marathon mouth. "Dude, you just asked me like four questions in one breath."

"Sorry if my brain thinks twice as fast as yours. Let me ask them one at a time so you can understand. Was Annie seriously hurt?"

"She has a concussion, two broken ribs, and a messed up shoulder," Cooper said. "She's pretty damn lucky, if you ask me, considering her car flipped over."

"Was she wearing her seat belt?"

"I'm sure she was, knowing Annie. She won't drive out of the driveway without putting it on."

"Question number two." Sean held up two fingers. "Did y'all break up?"

"Not officially, no."

"But it's in the works?"

"I don't know," Cooper said. "I guess."

Sean crossed his arms over his chest. "Who wants out, you or her?"

Cooper kept his eyes on the road. "I can't speak for her."

"So you're the one causing the problem. Are you crazy, Coop? The two of you had a good thing going. Annie is like seriously hot. You're not gonna find anyone better."

"I'm not looking for anyone better." Cooper waited for traffic in the oncoming lane to clear before making a left-hand turn. "My feelings for Annie haven't changed. My feelings about everything else in my life have."

Sean placed his hand over his chest. "That includes me. For

whatever reason. Don't think I haven't noticed. You and I haven't hung out together in months."

Cooper snuck a quick glance at his twin. Sean's face had grown serious. A rare expression for the fun-loving guy.

"It's not you, Sean. It's me. We're getting ready to go off to college. Everything is changing for us. The decisions we make now will affect the rest of our lives."

Sean threw up his hands. "I get it, bro. We can no longer be halves. Time to become whole."

Cooper smiled. "I hope that doesn't mean we'll no longer know what the other is thinking." He would miss this intuitive awareness he shared with his twin. The way they finished each other's sentences. The way they craved the same foods at the same time. The way they recognized when the other one was hungry or hurt or tired, oftentimes before the other twin realized it himself.

"There's no *we* about it. I can read you like a cheap novel. You, on the other hand, have no idea what I'm thinking." Sean looked away and stared out the window. "You're not being fair to Annie. You need to tell her how you feel."

Cooper pulled in behind the line of cars waiting to get into the student parking lot at Prospect High. "I can't very well break up with her now, while she's in the hospital."

"So instead, you're gonna let her lie there in that hospital bed, worrying about what she's done to make you push her away? Be fair, Coop. Annie is more than your girlfriend. She's family. If you're not careful, you'll be dealing with the wrath of Aunts Sam and Faith."

Sean was right. He'd rejected Annie for weeks. She'd have to be deaf, dumb, and blind not to suspect their relationship was ending. And she was none of the above. She was an amazing person who deserved to be treated with respect. Bare minimum, she deserved an explanation. So what was holding him back? Breaking up with Annie meant she'd be available to go out with other guys. Since neither of them had ever been in a relationship, the logical side of him understood they should date other people before they made a lifetime commitment. The selfish and irrational side, the part that encompassed his heart, couldn't bear the thought of her kissing another guy.

He'd marry Annie tomorrow if only he could figure out the rest of his life.

## EIGHT

## ELI

No matter how hard he tried, Eli could not get Thea Bell out of his mind. She was so young and pretty, with so much life ahead of her. And she seemed like a genuine, sweet girl, unlike her brothers. Thea reminded Eli of Flora, determined to remain positive despite the hardships they encountered. Why did some folks have to fight their way through life when others had it so easy?

Poor Flora, barely in her forties and stricken by the worst kind of diabetes, the type that claimed limbs and caused kidneys to fail. Working at The Grill had contributed to her obesity and complicated her medical condition. A year ago, when she could no longer keep up with her work, Al Carter, the manager at The Grill, had been forced to let her go. He had given her a generous severance package. As far as Eli knew, that was unheard of in the restaurant industry. He assumed that that money was long gone and that Flora was currently collecting unemployment.

The challenges Flora dealt with at home did little to alleviate her stress. Her two sons, Thea's older brothers by at least ten years, were the reasons she was destined for an early grave. Flora had pleaded with Eli, time and time again, to help her sons.

"They good boys at heart. They just need a little guidance." Flora and Eli both knew that wasn't true. Tyrone and Willie were her sons. Naturally, she wanted to believe the best about them. But the Bell brothers were pure evil. They'd beat up on an old lady if they thought they could get something out of her.

Eli hadn't seen the Bell brothers in several months. He'd heard rumors that Tyrone and Willie had left town. Which is why he'd been so surprised when Thea had mentioned they were still around. Which is why he nearly choked on his tuna fish sandwich when he saw them slumming outside the Minute Mart not twenty-four hours after he met their baby sister in the emergency room. A gnawing feeling in his gut warned him that this next chapter with the Bell boys would not end well.

He stuffed the rest of the sandwich in his mouth and removed his binoculars from his center console. He was parked in front of the public library directly across the street from the convenience store, and had a clear view of the brothers. When a female—attractive, late twenties, sandy hair, and curves in all the right places—approached the entrance to the store, Tyrone stepped in front of her to prevent her from opening the door. When she tried to go around him, he stepped sideways, blocking her path. They shuffled back and forth several times, a modified side-step dance. She planted her fists on her hips and mouthed something to Tyrone that Eli couldn't hear. Tyrone took a step toward the woman, shortening the space between them. When he placed his hand on her waist, she brought her leg up and kneed him in the groin. Tyrone doubled over in pain. Despite his closed window and the distance between them, Eli could hear the wounded man's string of expletives.

He jumped out of his patrol car and darted across the street. "Here, let me help you inside." He held the door open for the woman, and then entered the convenience store behind her. "Are you okay?"

"I'm better off than he is." She jutted her chin at Tyrone.

Eli chuckled. "He got what he deserves, no doubt about it. I saw for myself just how capable you are of protecting yourself, but for my own peace of mind, I'll wait outside and walk you to your car."

She nodded. "I'd appreciate that."

Eli stepped back outside. He'd have a difficult time telling the Bell brothers apart if not for their hairstyles and Tyrone's two gold front teeth. Both were short, lean, and scrappy. Tyrone preferred cornrows while Willie wore his hair in a low tapered Afro. They were always dressed in Nike athletic apparel—black running pants and Dri-FIT shirts with short sleeves, despite the weather, to show off their bulging biceps.

Taking Tyrone by the arm, he dragged him out of the way of the door so other customers could enter. "I'd say that woman taught you a good and proper lesson."

"I don't know what you're talking about," Tyrone said through clenched teeth, his face still pinched in pain.

"As a matter of fact, I do. I witnessed the whole thing from across the street." Eli gestured at his patrol car. "What's wrong with you, harassing an innocent woman like that?"

"You need to get your eyes checked, pig. She came onto me. Didn't she, Willie?"

His brother offered a one-shoulder shrug in response. "S'up, Eli," he said, with an upward head nod. "I ain't seen you in a while."

"I was just thinking the same thing about you, Willie. I'd heard rumors the two of you had split town. It's unfortunate for the innocent, law-abiding citizens of Prospect that you're still here."

Tyrone puffed out his chest. "Sorry to disappoint you, bruh. But you can't get rid of us that easy."

The woman exited the store with a Diet Coke and a pack of Lance Toast Chee Crackers. "I'm parked right there," she said to

Eli, pointing out a red late-model Beetle two spaces over. "You don't need to walk with me."

"In that case, I'll watch from here." He tipped his hat at her. "You have a nice day, now. And sorry for the trouble." He kept his eyes on her while she made her way to her car. Once she had driven off, Eli turned back to the Bell brothers. "Y'all run along now. Go find yourselves somewhere else to hang out. If I catch you around here again, I'll charge you with loitering."

"We're leaving anyway, bruh," Tyrone said, shuffling backward down the sidewalk. "Oh wait." He stopped walking. "I forgot to ask. How's Annie? My sister's all tore up about her accident yesterday."

*Why the little prick? How dare he mention Annie's name. Eli wondered whether* Tyrone was taunting him to get a rise out of him, or whether he was making some kind of threat against his family. Anger surged through his body, but he gritted his teeth and forced himself to remain calm. The worst thing he could do was let Tyrone see that he'd gotten to him. "Annie's fine. Thanks for asking," he said, and strolled across the street to his patrol car.

He drove straight back to the station where he spent the next hour combing through the recent reports on the Bell brothers. They'd been charged with a handful of misdemeanors apiece, most relating to dealing drugs and illegal firearms. In addition, there were the assault charges brought against Willie by a former girlfriend and the armed robbery Tyrone was questioned about. Somehow, someway, they'd managed to avoid jail time. Eli suspected they were up to their scrawny little necks in all of the above and a hell of a lot more.

"Watch out, you slimy bastard," Eli said to Tyrone's mug shot on the computer monitor. "I'm coming after you. And when I catch you, I'm gonna put you in jail for a very long time."

## NINE

ANNIE

M ike was waiting in Annie's room when she returned from having her CT scan.

"Eli tracked your belongings down for you." He raised his arms, holding her bag in one hand and her Chuck Taylors in the other. He removed her cell phone from the pocket of his scrubs. "Believe it or not, your phone survived the accident."

She took the phone from him. "It still has some battery left," she said, thumbing through the texts, none of them from Cooper. She set the phone on the bed table. "Where's Faith?"

"Bitsy's not feeling well. She went to pick her up from school."

Annie wrinkled her brow. "I hope it's nothing serious."

"Nah." Mike waved away her concern. "Just a tummy ache. She had a playdate yesterday afternoon followed by a sleepover last night. Remember, she's never spent the night out before. And on a school night . . . It was probably too much for her. I'm sure she's gonna want to come see you though."

Annie caught sight of her reflection in the mirror over the sink. Her face was pale with dark circles under her eyes. Never mind the bandage covering most of her forehead. She looked like a mummy. "Do you think she should? I don't want to scare her."

"I'm not worried about Bitsy. She's tougher than we give her credit for."

Annie smiled. "True." She'd grown to think of the spirited seven-year-old as her little sister. "Did Faith tell you about the little talk we had earlier? About Thea."

"She mentioned it."

"I don't see why she's so worried. My life has been different from most girls my age, Mike. I can take care of myself. It's not fair for Faith to start picking my friends for me. I haven't had many friends, actually. And Thea is a good person."

Mike moved to the edge of his seat. "I think maybe you misunderstood, honey. Eli knows Thea's family. He's had several run-ins with her older brothers. Faith wanted you to be aware of the situation, to warn you that the Bell home might not be safe. She doesn't have anything against Thea. Faith loves you very much. She doesn't want to see anything happen to you. She's overprotective. And I can't say I blame her after everything Bitsy has been through, being abused by her father and the kidnapping last summer."

"That makes sense, I guess." Annie's chin quivered and her eyes filled with tears. She looked away. Why had she automatically assumed the worst of Faith, who had never been anything but supportive of her? And why did she burst into tears at the smallest things these days? It was all Cooper's fault. Why didn't he just go ahead and break up with her? Blowing her off with the silent treatment wasn't Cooper's style. Or maybe it was and she didn't know him as well as she thought she did. "Am I going to need surgery on my shoulder?"

"More than likely. You have a fractured clavicle, aka your collarbone. The bones are displaced, which means the orthopedist will need to use a plate and screws to hold them together while they heal. The CT scan will show if there is any other damage to the ligaments in that area." Mike removed a tissue from the box on the bed table and handed it to her. "I don't want you to worry. We have the best orthopedist in town on the case. Faith and I will see you through this. Before you know it, your shoulder will be as good as new."

Annie blew her nose. "That's good, I guess."

Standing, Mike went to the computer cart in the corner. His fingers flew across the keyboard as he accessed her chart. "Your vitals are strong. I see they've altered your meds a little. How's your pain, on a scale of one to ten?"

"Seven. I'm more aware of my shoulder than I was earlier."

He walked back to the bed and sat down gently beside Annie. "Do you remember being in the emergency room last night?"

Annie suddenly found it difficult to breathe. *What he really wants to know is whether I remember him questioning me about being pregnant.* In a shaky voice, she replied, "It's all kind of blurry."

"I'm not sure if you remember it, but I asked you if there was any chance you might be pregnant. Before I order X-rays for my patients, I'm required to ask women of childbearing years that question. When you responded yes, we checked the hormone levels in your blood. You are, in fact, pregnant. Do you have any idea how far along you might be?"

Her heart pounded against her ribs. "It only happened once, on New Year's Eve. We got carried away. It scared both of us, and we haven't done it again since. Did you tell Faith?"

"You asked me not to. I'll let you tell her when you're ready," Mike said, smoothing out the blanket. "I'm sure this comes as a shock to you, honey, an unexpected bend in the road. But you can count on Faith and me to support you. Together, we will explore your options and come up with a solution that works best for you."

Annie rolled her eyes. "What options? I'm going to have a

baby. Just like my mother. Knocked up and washed up before I'm twenty. In my case, before I'm even eligible to vote."

"It's my responsibility, as a doctor and your legal guardian, to point out your options. Adoption and abortion are among them. I see teenage mothers in the ER every day. These young mothers are still girls. Children having children. Healthwise, they are usually as bad off as their babies. You and Cooper have your whole lives ahead of you. You need to consider what is best for your future."

"Leave Cooper out of it!"

Mike jerked his head back at the anger in her voice. "I'm sorry. You mentioned New Year's Eve. I just assumed the baby is his."

Annie's face beamed red. "Of course the baby is his. Whose else would it be?" Blinking away the tears, she stared up at the bank of monitors over her head. "Never mind, Mike. I need to let this sink in before I worry about Cooper. It's my body, not his."

"Which is why we need to take one thing at a time. Let's deal with the shoulder first. Then, after you've been home for a couple of days and are feeling more like yourself, we'll tell Faith. She loves you, you know. As do Sam and Jackie."

Annie brought her good hand to her bandaged forehead. "I forgot about Jackie. She's gonna freak. Promise me you won't tell her, Mike. Or Cooper or Sam or anybody. No one can know about this until I decide what to do. Please!"

"Shh, now." He rubbed her knee beneath the blanket. "You can trust me. I won't say a word until you're ready to talk about it with the others."

She sniffled. "Thank you."

The door banged open and Bitsy came skipping into the room. Annie winced in pain when the little girl leapt onto the bed and snuggled up to her.

Faith rushed to her side. "Bitsy, honey, you need to be gentle with Annie. She's got a lot of boo-boos."

"She's fine." Annie kissed the top of Bitsy's head. "But you need to lie still, kiddo. Okay?"

"Okay," Bitsy said, stretching her body out as straight and rigid as a two-by-four. "What happened to your head, Annie? Mama said you had an accident. Did you fall down the stairs at school? A girl in the other second grade class fell down the stairs at my school and broke her arm. Is your arm broken?" Bitsy's hazel eyes searched for Annie's.

Annie smiled. She loved this kid. If only she could go back to being seven years old again, to have someone else taking care of her, when all she had to worry about was what doll she wanted to play with. Only Annie had never owned any dolls. And she'd never really had anyone to take care of her. Aside from her father. And he'd tried. They'd gotten along as best they could. While he wasn't as smart or educated or capable as Mike, he'd been every bit as loving. But her father was no stand-in for the mother she dreamed of. The other kids at the different schools she'd attended all had mothers. She'd never understood why she was different from them. She prayed every night for her mother to return. Would she look and act like the other mothers? The mothers wearing yoga clothes and big sunglasses, driving SUVs as big as the yachts docked at the marinas where her father worked. The mothers who came to read to her class during lunchtime. The mothers who packed the auditorium for musicals and plays and awards ceremonies.

Annie hugged Bitsy tight. "It's my shoulder, Bitsy. Not my arm. And I didn't fall down the stairs. I was in a car accident."

Bitsy's mouth formed an O. "Did you run a red light and hit another car?"

"No, squirt. Come here." Mike lifted the tiny girl off the bed and cradled her in his arms. "The accident wasn't Annie's fault. It was just one of those things that sometimes happens. But it's nothing for you to worry about. Okay?" He tickled her until she squealed, "Okay." He covered her mouth with his hand until she quieted down.

"Annie looks like she could use a nap," Faith said. "How about we go down to the cafeteria for an ice cream cone?"

Bitsy flung her arms in the air. "Yay. Can we bring one back for Annie?"

TEN

HEIDI


Heidi was rolling out biscuits on the kitchen island—prepping for a seated dinner for fifty people, a thirtieth wedding anniversary celebration for one of her new clients—when Hugh called. "Can you get away for a few minutes? I have something I want to show you." The excitement in his voice caught her attention.

"Now? I'm up to my elbows in biscuit dough." She scratched her nose with the back of her hand, leaving behind a smudge of flour. "I don't mean to sound ungrateful. I love my kitchen, which is really *your* kitchen, of course, but preparing for an event takes twice as long as it would in a commercial kitchen."

"I may have the solution to your problem," he said.

"Please tell me you're considering installing another oven in my apartment."

He chuckled. "No. What I want to show you is better. It won't take long. Thirty minutes tops."

Her interest piqued, she set the rolling pin down and flicked on the oven light, peeking inside at the cake layers that were just beginning to rise. "Can you give me an hour?"

"I'll text you the address," he said, and ended the call.

Heidi had made a string of bad choices when it came to men. But so far, everything indicated that Hugh was a keeper. He was the one positive thing that had happened to her since she'd moved back to South Carolina from California. Reconciling with her daughter hadn't been as easy as she'd hoped, and her catering was taking off slower than she'd planned. Although she had several weddings on the horizon, her business did not compare to the success she'd experienced in Beverly Hills where her clients booked their events months, sometimes a year, in advance. She was proud of her resume. But no one in the Lowcountry seemed to care about the glitzy over-the-top affairs she'd arranged in Hollywood. She needed a presence in Charleston—a storefront on one of the prominent streets where she offered specialty items and gourmet takeout in the front with a commercial kitchen for catering in the back. But she needed to act soon. Her savings account was dwindling, taking her self-esteem with it.

Hugh was waiting for her in front of the converted warehouse with a man at least a foot taller and twenty years younger than he was. Based on the awkward manner in which he introduced himself, Heidi thought the realtor as green as the first blades of grass in the springtime. But Ken Cook spoke of Charleston architecture and the commercial real estate market with confidence and expertise. After reciting the history of the building and offering a brief overview of the neighborhood, he unlocked the front door, stepping aside for them to enter the mid-nineteenth-century cotton warehouse.

The concrete floors were made to look old, but the wooden ceilings, exposed beams, and brick walls were original. Heidi took in the natural light streaming through the windows. "It reminds me of Sam's place in Prospect—Captain Sweeney's Seafood. Only their showroom is cold and sterile with white walls and subway tile. It works for seafood but I prefer this warm and cozy feeling for my business."

Ken led them to the kitchen in the back. "The appliances are top-of-the-line commercial grade. As you can see, they're practically new."

Heidi ran her fingers across the stainless steel countertops and peeked inside the commercial-sized ovens. "How did you stumble upon this place?" she asked Hugh.

"A client friend of mine is in the market for retail space—either women's clothing or shoes, I can't remember which. He asked me to check out the plumbing and electrical." Hugh spread his arms wide. "Removing all this was not cost effective for his purposes, even if he resold the appliances and fixtures."

Heidi turned to Ken. "What was here before, a restaurant?"

He nodded. "A Thai franchise owned by a group on the West Coast. The food wasn't bad but the local staff mismanaged the place."

"And how much are they asking?" Heidi asked.

Ken produced a glossy flyer that outlined the specifics. When she saw the price, Heidi shut her green eyes tight, and then opened them wide again. "Whoa! This is way out of my league." She handed the flyer back to him. "I'm sorry, but we're wasting your time."

He held up his hand, refusing to take the flyer. "Keep it. The building has been on the market for several months and the owner is motivated to sell. The whole second floor is unfinished. You could convert it into office or living space. The rent might help compensate for the price. Would you like to see it?"

Heidi considered the convenience of living and working in the same building, and the money she could save on the pricey rent she paid Hugh. She mentally calculated the amount she would need for the deposit and the balance she would have to borrow from the bank. Even if she made a low-ball offer and the seller accepted, she would still fall far short. "I don't think so. Not today."

Ken removed his cell phone from his pocket. "I'll tell you what. I'm going to step outside and make a phone call. Why don't you take your time and look around. Give it some thought." Before Heidi could object, he turned his back on them and left the kitchen.

She turned to Hugh. "Why did you do this to me? You knew I'd fall in love with this place."

"Because this place is perfect for you. Look." He opened the back door wide. "An alleyway leads to this small parking lot where you can load up your van and have deliveries brought in."

She'd recently purchased a used utility van to transport her food and supplies to events. She stuck her head out the door, taking in the small asphalt lot that was sectioned off in neat parking spaces. "That's convenient. But not a deal breaker."

Hugh closed the back door and opened another that led to a generous-size storage room. "There's plenty of room in here for all your *stuff*," he said with emphasis on the last word.

She smiled. Hugh teased her constantly about the entertainment ware she had stored in her spare bedroom and in the back of the van. She stepped into the closet and tried to picture her plates, trays, and stemware organized neatly on the shelves. "I can't argue that the place is perfect. Unfortunately, the price is not."

Heidi returned to the front of the warehouse. Circling the showroom, she imagined an old pine farm table set with linens and tableware under the front window and wine racks lining the back wall. She would position commercial refrigerators and coolers along the other walls, featuring gourmet carryout dinners, appetizers, sides, and salads. The center of the room would house metal shelves packed with specialty items flown in from California and around the world. She would hire a graphic artist to design the logo. She imagined the initials *H* and *A* intertwined, painted across the window, *Heidi and Annie, Catering for Every Occasion.*

Hugh approached her from behind and wrapped his arms

around her waist. "What do you think? Shall we take a look upstairs?"

She leaned back against him, feeling the tickle of his breath against her neck. "I don't know, Hugh. I'm tempted. I have the money for the down payment. But I doubt the bank will finance the rest, not until my business income is more consistent. It might take me two or three years to get where I need to be."

He nibbled at her ear. "You wouldn't be buying the warehouse for your catering business alone. You would be opening up a gourmet food shop. All new businesses are risky. But you have a solid resume to support your expertise. You just need to convince the loan officer that you are capable."

She turned to him, taking his scruffy face in her hands. "You're a dear for being so supportive. Let me sleep on it for a couple of days. It's more complicated than just buying floor space. I would need to hire full-time employees. I could spend a fortune just outfitting this showroom with the proper equipment and fixtures. And that doesn't include the inventory." She sighed. "With everything that's going on with Annie, I can barely focus on this party tonight, let alone buying a warehouse."

"I can't believe you still haven't heard anything," Hugh said. "Did you call the hospital?"

"Yes. They rang Annie's room, but no one answered. They're restricted by the HIPAA law to give me any information on her condition."

"Which hardly seems right since you're her mother. Did you call Sam?"

"I've left several messages for Sam and Jackie. I understand they resent my interference, and considering the circumstances, I don't blame them, but I have a right to know how my daughter's doing. If I don't hear from them by tonight, I'm going to drive down to Prospect first thing in the morning."

COOPER

C ooper's mother texted him during his last period of the day, instructing him to meet her at the hospital after school.

He texted back: "*I was planning to work out after school.*"

Jackie: "*You can work out after you visit Annie.*"

Arguing with his mother was a waste of energy: "*Fine.*"

Jackie was waiting for him in the main hospital lobby, the streamers from a bouquet of balloons tied around her wrist. They walked down the hall and around the corner to the elevators. She turned to him once they were inside. "Cooper, honey, whether you make up with her or break up with her, you need to be fair to Annie for the sake of the family."

The hairs on the back of his neck bristled. Had one of his aunts complained to his mother? "Did someone say something to you about Annie and me?"

"Not yet. But believe me, I will hear from Sam and Faith if you break Annie's heart. If you have to let her down, at least let her down gently."

"Okay, Mom. Jeez. I get it." He could no longer procrastinate what he'd been putting off for weeks. When the elevator door opened onto the third floor, he squared his shoulders and lifted his head high. He gathered courage as he paraded down the hall toward room 311, but when he saw Annie's small injured body lying in the big hospital bed, his confidence waned.

"Annie, sweetheart, you poor thing." Jackie tied the bouquet of balloons on the arm of a wooden chair and went to her side. She smoothed her hair back and kissed the part of her forehead that wasn't bandaged. "I'm so sorry you're having to go through all this."

Annie's brown eyes met his. "Hey."

"Hey, Annie." He fluttered his fingers at her and took a step back, away from this beautiful damaged creature.

"Have you gotten the results from the CT scan?" Jackie asked.

Annie winced in pain as she shifted in bed. "The orthopedist was here a few minutes ago. I couldn't begin to tell you what all is wrong with my shoulder. He scheduled the surgery for tomorrow morning. I should be able to go home tomorrow afternoon."

"That's great news," Jackie said. "Isn't it, Cooper?"

"Sure," he said, backing himself into the nearest corner.

Jackie plumped up Annie's pillow and tucked the cover under her chin. She flitted about the room, straightening the items on the bed table and reading the cards on the flower arrangements lined up on the shelf beneath the window. When she opened the blinds, Annie's hand flew to her eyes. "Please don't open that, Jackie. My eyes are sensitive to the light."

"I'm sorry, honey. I forgot about your concussion." Jackie closed the blinds and returned to the bed. "I'm not going to stay. I don't want to wear you out. I'm on my way to the store to get the ingredients for that chicken and corn chowder you love so much. I'll have some waiting for you as soon as you get home."

Annie rewarded Jackie with a half-hearted smile. "That sounds good. Thank you. And thank you for the balloons."

"You take care of yourself, now, and I'll see you after the

surgery." Jackie kissed Annie's head once more before exiting the room, leaving behind a trail of Chanel No. 5 on her way out.

Cooper, hoping his mother would take a hint and ditch that awful floral fragrance she'd always worn, had given her a perfume that smelled like lavender for Christmas one year. The package remained unopened on her dressing table.

"Aren't you going with her?" Annie asked.

Cooper followed her gaze to the door. "We drove here separately." He pushed off the wall and stepped closer to the bed. "You really banged yourself up good, Annie. How fast were you going?"

A surge of anger caused her head to throb. "The other driver crossed into my lane. I wouldn't have been able to stop the car in time no matter how fast I was driving." Turning her head away from him, Annie stared across the room at the whiteboard, where the name of the shift nurse and pertinent patient information was scrawled. "Did Jackie make you come?"

There was no sense in lying to her. Annie knew him too well. "I was going to visit you. Just not today."

"When, then?" she asked, still intent on the whiteboard. "Next month? Or were you planning to wait until the summer to break up with me? Clearly, you don't want to be with me anymore. What are you waiting for?"

"It's not you, Annie. It's me. I'm confused."

"That's lame, Cooper. A clichéd excuse if ever I've heard one. I think you owe me a better explanation than that."

"You're right. I do." He massaged the back of his neck. "Problem is, I don't really know how to explain this to you. I'm not the same person I was when we started dating two months ago. I've always known exactly what I wanted out of life until now. My future was clear, like looking out over the inlet on a cold cloudless day. But the fog has settled in."

"Are you talking about medical school, or are you talking about me?"

"Medical school . . . both . . . I'm not really sure. I know this much. I don't want to be a doctor anymore. And I don't want to live in a small town. I want to go where the action is, for whatever profession I choose. Sean has always been the competitive one. But I feel like a whole new world has opened up for me in graphic art. I'm obsessed. And excited. I want to see where this path leads me. With no strings attached."

A single tear spilled from Annie's right eye and traveled down her cheek. "I didn't mean to be a noose around your neck. I thought we were hanging out because we have a lot in common and enjoy each other's company."

"That's just it, Annie. We don't have as much in common as you think. I can never be happy living in Prospect. I want more than life here has to offer."

Annie's eyes turned cold. "Who said I wanted to live here forever? I like Prospect. For the first time in my life, I have a real family. I live in a real home. I'm no longer a poor fisherman's daughter destined to become a poor fisherman's wife. I have dreams too. Faith and Mike have taught me to believe in myself, that dreams do come true with hard work."

Cooper sat down on the mattress, careful not to touch her battered body. "I thought working at Sweeney's with Sam was your dream . . ."

"That's because you never asked." She jutted her chin out. "I want to travel the world, Cooper. See it all. I'd like to go to culinary school in New York, and then study for a few years in Italy. Maybe even France. After that, I hope to work at a five-star restaurant in a sophisticated city like New Orleans or San Francisco."

"What about Charleston?"

"And live in the same city as Heidi? No thanks." She picked at a loose thread on her blanket. "I guess we don't know each other so well after all."

Cooper hung his head. "I've missed being with you, Annie. Can we go back to being friends?"

"I'm sorry, but no. It's way too late for that. If only you'd trusted me with your feelings instead of ignoring me these past few weeks, things might have been different."

"I will always consider you my friend, Annie. If you ever need anything, you can count on me to be here for you. I don't want this to be the end for us. Just intermission."

TWELVE

HEIDI

S am, bundled up against the cold, was hurrying to her Jeep when Heidi pulled into the side parking lot at Captain Sweeney's Seafood Market on Friday morning. She tooted her horn, slid into the parking space next to Sam, and forced open the heavy door of her Mustang.

"I had to come," Heidi said as she approached Sam. "I'm sure I'm the last person you want to see, but I've been out of my mind with worry. How's Annie?"

Sam stiffened, drawing her Barbour coat tighter. "What, you mean no one called you? I thought Jackie said she would. Maybe I misunderstood."

"No!" Heidi said. "I haven't heard a word from anyone since I talked to you on Wednesday night. Please tell me she's okay."

"She's having surgery on her shoulder this morning." Sam glanced at her watch. "Now, in fact. Mike has the best orthopedist in town on her case. He'll repair the torn ligaments and put a plate and screws in to help mend the broken collarbone. He assures us she'll be fine."

"Whew!" Heidi collapsed against Sam's Jeep. "What a relief."

"I'm headed to the hospital now if you want to follow me over." Sam swept her arm toward Heidi's car.

A glint of hope appeared on Heidi's face, but quickly fell away. "Thanks anyway, but I'm not sure I'd be welcome."

Sam opened her car door and tossed her handbag inside. "Look, Heidi. We might as well put our cards on the table. I don't approve of the way you abandoned Annie when she was a baby. The irony of Allen leaving me and you leaving Allen has taken some time for me to process. More than anything I wanted to marry him and have a family with him, but none of that has anything to do with you. He left me long before he met you." She pointed at Heidi's chest. "We're humans. We make mistakes, especially when we're young. I only want what's best for Annie. It may take some time for her to sort out her feelings. Whether she decides to forgive you is up to her. But seeing that you and I are still friends can't hurt. It might even help."

"Do you mean it?" Heidi asked, feeling the weight of the world, at least the past sixteen years, lift off her shoulders.

"Of course I mean it." Sam looped her arm through Heidi's and steered her to her car. "Besides, I enjoy your company. I'd hate to lose one of the few girlfriends I have." She opened Heidi's door for her. "I'm warning you, though, Faith might not be such an easy sell."

---

When they arrived at the outpatient waiting room, Heidi and Sam were told that Faith was still in the back with Annie, that the doctor had experienced a delay and the patient had not yet gone into surgery.

"I don't know about you, but I could use some coffee," Sam said. "What say we go down to the cafeteria and see if we can find some."

They were pleased to discover a Starbucks kiosk in the

hospital cafeteria. They doctored their coffee with cream and sugar and found a table for two by the window. Sam removed her phone and thumbed a text. "I'll let Faith know where we are, in case she wants to join us."

"She'll be thrilled to see me, I'm sure." Heidi slipped off her coat, and draped it across the back of her chair. "Since we have a few minutes alone, do you mind if I ask you about your business? I've found an old converted warehouse. It's quite charming, actually. I'm considering opening a specialty market. Much like Sweeney's only geared toward my catering business instead of seafood."

Sam propped her elbows on the table. "That sounds exciting. Does the warehouse have a kitchen?"

Heidi nodded. "The current owner ran a Thai restaurant there. He had to close because of mismanagement. The appliances are practically new. I would operate my catering business out of the back and sell tableware, wine, gourmet foods, and specialty goods from all around the world out of the storefront."

Sam lifted her coffee cup to her lips. "Why bring in items from around the world when you have so many wonderful choices from right here in the Lowcountry?"

Heidi thought about the stoneground grits she loved so much and the Benne Wafers. She could have a whole section devoted to products from local vendors. "I haven't thought about that. But I like the idea. My goal is to have a place where folks can grab a salad for lunch or a casserole to take to a sick friend. I eventually plan to offer full dinners one or two days a week. Tell me, how many employees do you have?"

"Three full time—Roberto in the back, Mom out front, and one floater. That's me. We have two part-time—Annie, who comes in after school and helps wherever I need her, and Faith, who handles our accounting. Although Faith pitches in wherever we need her when we're shorthanded. I beef up the staff in the summertime and during the holidays. Right now, business is really slow. Being in downtown Charleston, I imagine you'll need more full-time employees."

"That's what I figured. And I will need extra staff to handle the catering events." Heidi blew on her coffee before taking a tentative sip. "The timing is all wrong for me. I have enough for the down payment, and the warehouse is the perfect space. I would feel more comfortable if I had a larger client base on the catering end. Then again, if I had a commercial kitchen, I could handle more than one event at a time."

"Hmm," Sam said, staring up at the ceiling. "Have you considered taking on an investor?"

Heidi gave Sam a quizzical look. "You know, that's a great suggestion. But I'm not sure where I would find one of those."

Sam folded her arms on the table. "How about me? I inherited some money from Uncle Mack, who wasn't really my uncle but that's a long story for another day. It's just sitting in the bank earning interest. I would love to put it to good use."

"I don't know, Sam," Heidi said in a weary tone of voice. "I'm not sure I like the idea of doing business with a friend. I would feel horrible if my project didn't succeed."

"That's why I would only invest a portion of my inheritance." Sam settled back in her chair and crossed her legs. "Why don't we both give it some thought. There might be economical benefits to a partnership of sorts. For starters, we would have more buying power with the wine distributor."

*We? Partnership? I thought we were talking about an investment.* But the idea of working closely with Sam appealed to her just the same. Heidi would benefit from Sam's vast experience operating a similar-type business. She admired Sam's spunk and her strong work ethic. Plus, with her only child off at college, she would have time to devote to their *partnership.*

Faith appeared in the doorway. She spotted them and marched over to their table. Tipping her head in Heidi's direction, she said, "What is she doing here?"

ASHLEY FARLEY

Of the three sisters, Faith was the one Heidi knew the least. She'd heard all about how considerate and even-tempered Faith was despite her unfortunate history with her abusive first husband. But Heidi had yet to see this favorable side of the youngest Sweeney sister. She'd been in her presence only once or twice, but each time Faith had come across as standoffish despite Heidi's attempts at friendliness.

"What'd you think, Faith?" Sam said. "She's here for Annie."

"She has no right to be here." Faith spoke with her back to Heidi, as though she wasn't in the room. "She's the one who put Annie in the hospital in the first place."

Sam rolled her deep blue eyes. "You're being melodramatic. Heidi and Annie had a disagreement. It happens everyday."

Faith's face turned scarlet. "It was more than a disagreement. Heidi antagonized poor Annie. She's been harassing her for weeks, calling her all the time and showing up out of the blue."

Sam stood to face her sister. "What on earth is wrong with you? You're not usually one to butt your nose in other people's business. Step aside, and let the two of them work out their relationship."

Faith clenched her fists. "I refuse to let that woman toy with Annie's emotions. I've been more of a mother to Annie in the past six months than Heidi's been in nearly seventeen years." Faith turned to Heidi. "I want you to leave. Now. Annie doesn't want you here. She's made that perfectly clear. If you continue to harass her, I'll file for a restraining order."

Heidi shot to her feet. "Go ahead and try. You won't get very far. I'm Annie's biological mother. The law is on my side. I made a mistake in leaving Annie when she was a baby. I intend on making it up to her now. And you can't stop me."

"Why now, when she's finally happy? She has a family who loves and appreciates her. Don't take that away from her. Annie has led a difficult life, all because of you. She had to grow up way too fast. The past few years have been especially hard on her,

68

having to take care of a sick father. And where were you during all this time? Out in Hollywood, kowtowing to the movie stars. There's nothing for you here, Heidi. Go back where you came from." Faith spun around and stormed out of the cafeteria.

"I'm so sorry," Sam said, watching her sister leave. "I don't know what's gotten into her. Clearly, she is under a lot of stress."

"Stress?" Heidi pointed at Faith's retreating figure. "That was more than stress. She has an anger management problem. I'm not sure she's stable enough to be raising my daughter."

THIRTEEN

ANNIE

Annie hated the way the medicine made her feel. She'd heard horrible stories about kids becoming addicted to narcotics. While she didn't want to become one of them, the pain in her shoulder was unendurable without it.

She cried all the time. And not just from the pain. Because of Heidi. Because of the accident. Because of Cooper. Because she was pregnant. Because her life was ruined.

She stayed in bed until she heard Faith, Mike, and Bitsy leave for church on Sunday morning. Until the hunger pains drove her to the kitchen for a bowl of cereal. She hated being hungry all the time. Painkillers suppressed the appetite for most people. But not her. She was as hungry as she'd ever been. Which was saying a lot. As a child, there'd been times when she'd gone twenty-four hours without a morsel of food. She'd already gained ten pounds since coming to Prospect. Soon, she would be fat. When the image of her pregnant body in a bikini came to mind, she lay her head on the table beside her cereal bowl and wept.

The doorbell rang sometime later. Ten minutes perhaps or it could've been thirty. She wasn't sure how long she'd been indulging herself in her pity party. She got up and plodded to the door, relieved to see Thea through the peephole.

"Is it safe for me to be here?" Thea slipped her hands inside her coat pocket and shifted her weight between her feet. "I figured your family might be at church. I get the impression they don't like me."

"Don't take it personally. It's your brothers they're worried about." Annie looked past Thea at the rusted Oldsmobile in the driveway. "Whose car is that?"

"That's my mama's. It's been in the shop for six months. My brothers finally sprang to get it fixed. It's older than me, but who cares as long as it gets me where I need to be."

Annie opened the door wider for Thea to come in. "Sounds like your brothers aren't all bad."

"They're mean as hornets, don't get me wrong. But my mama loves them anyway," Thea said as she trailed Annie to the kitchen. "And I appreciate however much or little they do for us."

"I understand," Annie said. "We don't get to pick our family."

"You got to pick Faith and Mike, didn't you?" Thea said, hand on hip.

"That's not the same thing and you know it. I certainly didn't pick Heidi." Annie held up a box of Cheerios. "Do you want some cereal?"

"No. But I wouldn't mind a cup of coffee." Annie returned to the table while Thea helped herself to a Donut House K-Cup from the carousel. She popped the pod into the machine and waited for it to brew. "So . . . how're you feeling?"

"All these meds make me feel funky," Annie said, "but I can't bear the pain without them."

"You should be able to get off of them soon," Thea said, spooning sugar into her coffee. "Have you made a decision about your problem?"

"Not really. All I know is that I don't want to have a baby. Which leaves only one option." Annie couldn't bring herself to say the word. Even the thought of terminating the pregnancy brought tears to her eyes.

Thea brought her coffee over to the table and sat in the chair opposite Annie. "Are you sure? Maybe you should take a few more days to think about it. Painkillers can mess with your head sometimes."

Annie used her napkin to mop her eyes. "Painkillers or not, I've never been more sure about anything in my life," she said with more conviction than she felt.

"Have you told Faith and Mike? You'll need their permission to have the procedure."

"Mike said he'd support whatever decision I make. I haven't even told Faith I'm pregnant yet. She's going to freak out."

"She's not gonna be happy about the situation, for sure. But from everything you've told me about Faith, I'd think she'd be understanding."

Annie sat back in her chair. "Not about this. Faith can't have any more children. And she's desperate for another baby.

"Oh. I see." Thea blew on her coffee before taking a sip.

"She's too nice to say it, but I know she'll be thinking how unfair it is that I got pregnant without even trying. My guess is she'll try to force me to have the baby, even if I put it up for adoption."

"You could talk to Heidi," Thea suggested. "I bet she'd help you. She'd do anything to get you to forgive her."

Annie snorted. "I'd rather have quadruplets and raise them on my own than ask Heidi for a favor."

Thea took another sip of her coffee. "What does Cooper think?"

Annie wrapped her good arm across her belly. "I haven't told him. And I'm not going to. It's over between us. There's no point dragging him into it."

Thea blinked hard, her long lashes fluttering over her golden eyes. "He's the baby daddy, girlfriend. You can't just not tell him."

"Yes, I can. Cooper made it clear that he doesn't want any strings attaching him to Prospect. Not me, and certainly not a baby."

"But the baby is half his. He has a right to know about it."

"That's not the way I see it." Annie looked away, staring out of the window at the dark clouds rolling in across the inlet. "It's not his body. He's not the one getting fat or giving up his dreams. People aren't gonna stare at him in the hallway at school and treat him like some freak." The thought of it made her want to throw up. She turned to her friend. "I don't mean to be rude, Thea. I appreciate you coming over. But I'm not feeling so well. Do you mind showing yourself out?"

"Of course. I understand." Thea pushed back from the table and walked her coffee cup to the sink. "You can call me anytime. If you need anything. When you're feeling better, now that I have wheels, we can hang out, maybe get a pizza or go to the movies."

Annie smiled. "That sounds nice, Thea. Thanks."

Mike found Annie still sitting at the kitchen table, stirring her milk around her cereal bowl, when he arrived home from church thirty minutes later. "Hey, kiddo. You look like you could use a friend." He loosened his tie, and pulled up a chair beside her. "Are you still in a lot of pain?"

"I can handle it." Annie searched the empty hallway behind him. "Where's Faith?"

"She and Bitsy are changing out of their church clothes. Is there something you want to talk to me about?"

Annie tore off tiny pieces of her napkin, balled them up, and rolled them into a pile in front of her. "I don't want to have this baby, Mike. Will you help me . . . you know, terminate the pregnancy?"

Mike set his pale eyes on her. "Are you sure that's what you want?"

She nodded, biting down on her quivering lip.

"Then I will help you. But only if Faith agrees."

73

"Come on, Mike," Annie said, smacking the palm of her good hand against the table. "We don't need to drag Faith into this. She'll go ballistic."

He sighed. "Faith hasn't been herself lately. I won't argue with that. But I can't, in good conscience, keep something like this from her." He paused for a minute, thinking. "Listen, Eli is working today and Sam is bringing Angelo's pizza over for lunch. Why don't I occupy Bitsy while you talk to Sam and Faith? Sam's presence will help soften the blow. And I think you might benefit from her perspective, since she was once in a situation similar to yours."

Even so, Annie dreaded having to confess to the two sisters the circumstances in which she found herself. She narrowed her eyes at Mike. "Is there anything I can say to get you to change your mind?"

"No, honey. I'm sorry. I'm doing what's best for you, even though you may not see it that way."

"Fine, then. Thanks for nothing." She got up from the table and stormed off to her room.

---

Annie listened to the voices drifting down the hallway from the kitchen to her bedroom. Mike and Bitsy, Sam and Faith. Laughing and chatting and carrying on, enjoying a Sunday meal together. What a shame she would soon ruin their day. When it sounded as though they'd finished eating, when the talk turned to afternoon chores and the impending winter storm, she ventured to the kitchen. She nodded a greeting to them, slapped a slice of pizza on a plate, and retreated to the adjoining family room.

Mike stood up from the table and stretched. "Say, Bits. Why don't you and I take Snowflake back to my bedroom and turn on a movie?"

Bitsy, cradling the puppy in her arms, bounced up and down

in her chair. "Can we watch *Frozen*?"

"I think *Frozen* is a fine choice for a stormy winter's afternoon." He scooped up the little girl and her puppy, and carried them from the room.

Sam and Faith cleared the table and loaded the dishwasher before joining Annie on the sofa. "Looks to me like someone's feeling better." Sam tucked a strand of Annie's greasy hair behind her ear. "The color has returned to your cheeks."

"I have great news," Faith said. "Relatively speaking, of course. I've been communicating with the insurance company. They have declared your car totaled."

"How is that good news?" Annie asked.

"Well . . ." Placing her arm on the back of the sofa, Faith shifted her position to face Annie. "For a car that suffered as much damage as yours, oftentimes when you have it repaired, the car never functions quite right again. This way the insurance company will write us a check for the full retail value of the car, so we can buy a new one. We'll go car shopping as soon as you're feeling better."

*Buy me a new car after I totaled the other one?* Annie knew enough about insurance to understand Faith and Mike's premium would go way up. She didn't deserve their kindness. She burst into tears.

"Oh, honey, what's wrong?" Faith rested a hand on Annie's trembling back.

"I'm pregnant!" she bawled.

Faith retracted her hand as though she'd been scalded. "What did you just say?"

Annie sobbed harder. "I said I'm pregnant. And I'm too young to have a baby. My life is ruined."

Annie felt Sam's body go rigid beside her. She risked a glance in Faith's direction. But Faith's pained expression was more than she could bear. She turned away, and that's when she noticed Bitsy in the doorway.

*How long has she been standing there?*

Annie swiped at her tears. "Do you need something, squirt?" she asked, sniffling.

Bitsy popped her thumb in her mouth, a gesture Annie had not seen the little girl do in months. "Snowflake needs to go outside," Bitsy said around her thumb. "I tried to wake Mike up but he's snoring."

"Then take her outside," Faith said.

Bitsy cringed at her mother's angry voice. "Yes, ma'am," she said, removing the thumb from her mouth and wiping it on her corduroys.

"But put your coat on. And be quick about it. It's cold outside."

The child scurried away with Snowflake nipping at her heels. Annie sat with Faith and Sam in an awkward silence until Bitsy returned five minutes later.

"Can I stay in here with you?" Bitsy asked.

"I'm sorry, sweetheart, but we are having grown-up time," Faith said in a softer voice. "Put the puppy up"—she pointed at Snowflake's crate—"and go back to my room with Mike."

"Fine." Bitsy did as she was told and stomped off down the hallway.

"What does Cooper think of all this?" Sam asked.

"He doesn't know I'm pregnant," Annie said. "He broke up with me. I've made up my mind to terminate the pregnancy. Mike says he'll help me as long as the two of you agree."

Sam and Faith exchanged a look Annie couldn't interpret.

Faith left the sofa and began pacing back and forth in front of the coffee table. "Abortion isn't your only option. You can put the baby up for adoption or you can keep it. Mike and I will help you raise it."

"I'm only sixteen years old. I'm not ready to be a mother."

Faith held her chin high. "Maybe you should have thought

about that before you had unprotected sex." She turned her back on them and left the room.

"It was an accident!" Annie called after her. She winced at the pain in her ribs when she shifted toward Sam. "It only happened once, I promise. It was New Year's Eve and we got caught up in the moment. We had no idea what we were doing, and it freaked us out so bad, we haven't done it again." More tears spilled from Annie's eyes.

Sam went to the kitchen and returned with a handful of napkins. "There, now," she said, wiping the tears from Annie's face. "It may seem like it, but this is not the end of the world. A baby doesn't have to ruin your life. Jamie and I are living proof of that."

"That's hardly a fair comparison, Sam. You were a lot older than me when you had Jamie. Look at Heidi. She was only twenty. And she ditched me because she couldn't handle the stress." She blew her nose into the napkin. "Why would I want to have a baby when I can't even take care of myself? Am I supposed to support it by working part-time at Sweeney's?"

"I'm not trying to convince you to keep the baby. I just want you to realize you have other options. Terminating the pregnancy is so final. I'd hate for you to make a hasty decision you might later regret." Sam patted Annie's thigh. "Take some time to think about it. I'm here for you, whenever you need to talk. I'll help you explore your options and support you whichever way you decide."

"Thank you." Annie rested her head against Sam. "Faith is so mad at me."

"She's not mad at you, Annie. She loves you. All of us do. And none of us want to see you suffer. You have to understand how hard this is for Faith, how unfair the situation must seem to her."

"Trust me, I get it," Annie murmured. "Nothing in my life has ever been fair."

## FOURTEEN

## FAITH

Faith removed her coat from the hall closet and slammed the front door behind her on the way out. She pulled her hood up, and ducked her head against the frozen drizzle that had begun to fall over the area. She inhaled deep breaths of icy air and started off down the driveway. When she reached the road, she increased her pace and headed north toward town. Forcing all thoughts of Annie's unwanted pregnancy from her mind, she focused on the burn in her thighs and the ache in her chest. She contemplated the chores waiting for her at home—the basket of laundry that needed folding, the stack of bills on her desk that needed to be paid, and the vegetable soup she'd planned to cook for dinner. A half mile down the road, when her muscles were relieved of tension, she allowed herself to open her mind to the idea of Annie having a baby.

Faith wasn't angry at Annie. The pregnancy had to be an accident. Annie was too cautious to let something like this happen out of carelessness. What upset and confused Faith was the bigger picture. Teenage girls got pregnant by accident every single day when so many women in good marriages with loving homes were barren. More than anything, she wanted to give Mike a baby. On

New Year's Eve, they'd had a heart-to-heart talk about their options for having more children. She'd stated her case for surrogacy, but he'd been adamantly opposed.

"I'm too old," Faith had argued when Mike mentioned adoption. "No adoption agency is going to give a baby to a forty-three-year-old mother." Mike was younger than Faith, but only by one year.

She still remembered his eager face. "It never hurts to try. All they can say is no."

They'd agreed to explore their options through private adoption agencies and Mike's connections at the hospital. So far, they hadn't gotten far on either count.

While the longing for a child was nearly unbearable—a visceral ache that took her breath away whenever she saw a pregnant woman or a woman carrying an infant—she wasn't sure she would survive rejection. Faith sensed Annie slipping away from her. And that alone felt like a knife slicing into her heart.

For seven blissful months, Annie had been her daughter in every way that mattered. Annie completed their family. She brought happiness to their lives with her buoyant personality, her seemingly endless talents, creativity, and resourcefulness. Faith hadn't lost her yet. But it was only a matter of time before Annie came to terms with her anger toward Heidi. They'd been close once, before Annie learned of Heidi's betrayal. Annie would eventually forgive Heidi and go live with her in Charleston.

Faith had turned around and was heading back home when Sam's Jeep pulled up beside her. The window rolled down. "There you are," Sam said, leaning across the passenger seat. "I've been looking everywhere for you. Get in! It's freezing out there."

Faith climbed into the Jeep, grateful for the warm air blowing on her feet.

"I need to run to the grocery store. Do you mind going with me?"

"That's fine. I have a couple of things I need to pick up as well." Faith patted her pockets. "Although I don't have my wallet with me."

"You can pay me back later." Sam eyed her cell phone in the cup holder. "But text your husband and tell him you're with me. He's worried sick."

Faith's fingers flew across the screen as she apologized to Mike for worrying him: *"Just needed some fresh air. Going to store with Sam. Back soon."*

"I hope you don't mind, but my grocery list is kinda long," Sam said as they headed toward town. "Eli and I are having the family over for dinner Tuesday night. I hope you can come. I can't wait for you to see what we've done to our living room. Our shipment of furniture finally arrived last week."

"Hmm, Tuesday." Faith tapped her chin. "Seems like we already have something on the calendar."

"Tuesday is Valentine's Day, Faith. Are you and Mike planning a date night?"

Faith's face lit up. "How could I forget Valentine's Day? No date night for us, though. Valentine's Day is for celebrating with all those you love, not just your significant other. Does your invitation include the children?"

Sam nodded. "Of course. Eli is cooking ribs on his new Green Egg."

A deep line creased Faith's forehead. "I'm sorry I ran out like that, back at the house. I hope Annie isn't too upset."

"She's upset. But not at you. Annie understands where you're coming from." Sam turned into the Harris Teeter parking lot and drove around until she found a space close to the door. "The weatherman says we may get an inch of ice. I bet there's not a loaf of bread left on the shelves."

They hopped out of the car and made a dash for the store. They each got a cart and shopped the crowded aisles for the items on their lists.

"Every child is a gift from God," Faith said as they waited in the long checkout line. "Terminating the pregnancy would be a mistake. I understand if she doesn't want to keep the baby. But she can give it to someone else to raise."

Sam smiled. "Like who, you?"

Faith's mouth dropped open. "Was that Annie's idea?"

"No. But I'm sure she's thought about it. We've all thought about it. Including you." Sam nudged Faith with her elbow. "Having you and Mike raise Annie's child is the most logical solution."

Sam paid for the groceries and they wheeled their bags to the car.

"I can think of a hundred reasons that scenario won't work," Faith said when they were on the way home. "The biggest is the friction it could potentially cause in our family. I would be raising Cooper's child as my own. How would Jackie feel about that? And Mom? She would never understand that arrangement. Seriously, Sam. That idea is just screwed up."

"Stranger things have happened. Especially these days. The traditional family unit no longer exists."

"Maybe so. But that doesn't mean it's the right choice for us." Faith stared out the window as she contemplated the idea. What was wrong with her? She wanted a baby more than anything, yet here she was thinking of every reason not to adopt the one that had fallen into her lap. "Think about the potential for heartache down the road. What if, in ten years, Annie decides she wants the baby back? Am I supposed to just hand the child over?"

"That won't happen if you hire an attorney and follow the proper procedures," Sam said, her eyes glued to the road.

"If Mike and I adopt the baby, Annie will leave this town and never come back. She's like a daughter to me. I don't want to lose her, anymore than I'm already losing her to Heidi."

"You're underestimating Annie. She has enough love in her heart for ten mothers and twenty children."

"I agree with you there." Faith turned to face Sam. "Okay,

then. What am I supposed to tell this child when he or she asks about his or her biological parents? Hey kid, your uncle is actually your biological father."

Sam snickered. "It won't come as a surprise if he or she has the same red hair and deep blue eyes as Cooper."

"I'm glad *you* think this is funny, because I'm not laughing." Faith sat back in her seat and crossed her arms over her chest. "Trust me, Sammie, your solution won't work. Do us all a favor and don't bring it up again."

FIFTEEN

ELI

Eli was purchasing a chicken salad croissant and a coffee from the Island Bakery early Tuesday afternoon when he spotted Willie and Tyrone Bell coming out of the liquor store next door. He hurried out to his cruiser, started the engine, and pulled into the line of traffic two cars behind the Bell brothers' silver, jacked-up Dodge Charger. Eli experienced a flash of anger, an emotion he'd long since learn to suppress, when he thought about the way Tyrone had hassled that young woman in front of the Minute Mart several days ago. He was determined to get these two off the streets of Prospect and send them to a maximum security prison for a very long time. Away from Annie. Away from Flora and Thea. He would build a rock-solid case against them, even if it meant following them around town until they slipped up. And they would eventually slip up. He felt that in his gut.

He realized that sending the brothers to prison would likely put Thea and Flora in financial hardship. But he would figure out a way to somehow compensate for the money Willie and Tyrone gave them, however meager and inconsistent their contributions were.

When the Charger sped through a red light, Eli turned on his blue lights, accelerated past the cars in front of him, and stayed close on the Charger's tail until they pulled over to the side of the road.

Eli got out of his cruiser and approached the other car. The tinted window rolled down and Tyrone flashed Eli a mouthful of gold teeth. "Dude. Eli. What's with the blue lights? I didn't do anything wrong."

"You sped through that red light back there." Eli aimed his thumb over his shoulder. "You could have killed someone if another car had been entering the intersection."

Willie's eyebrows shot up above his mirrored sunglasses. "A red light? Seriously, man. You know that light was yellow. You just looking to give us a hard time. I call this harassment."

"Call it what you want," Eli said. "You'll have a hard time proving it."

"C'mon, Deputy Fife," Tyrone said. "Can't you find someone else in Mayberry to pick on?"

Eli held out his hand, palm up, fingers wiggling. "License and registration, please." He kept a close eye on Tyrone's hands as he retrieved his license from his wallet and the registration from above the sun visor."

Tyrone slapped the credentials in Eli's hand. "What will it take for you to overlook my little mistake?" he asked, thumbing through the hundred-dollar bills in his wallet.

Eli peered at him over the top of his Ray Ban sunglasses. "Are you suggesting a bribe?"

"Call it whatever you want. Bottom line is, I get my way, and you get to take your lady out on the town. I'm guessing that uniform don't earn you much."

Willie cackled from the passenger seat.

Encouraged by his brother's laughter, Tyrone continued. "How long has it been since you treated Sam-an-tha to a romantic dinner?"

The sound of his wife's name on Tyrone's lips sent a wave of fury through Eli's body. He reached for the chrome handle and flung Tyrone's door open. "Step out of the car." Tyrone hesitated and Eli added, "Now!"

In exaggerated slow motion, Tyrone climbed out of the car. When he was finally on his feet, Eli grabbed a handful of Tyrone's Nike T-shirt and spun him around to face the car. "Place your hands on the roof and spread your legs." Eli patted him down, removing a switchblade from his back pocket. "What do we have here?"

"Ain't no law against carrying a knife, bro."

"If I had my way, you'd need a permit to own a butter knife." Eli stuffed the knife in his coat pocket. He wrenched Tyrone's hands behind his back and slapped a pair of handcuffs on his wrists.

"What up, man?" Tyrone said. "You can't arrest me."

"Like hell I can't. You tried to bribe an officer of the law." Eli manhandled Tyrone around to the other side of the car. He removed his revolver from its holster, and then aiming it at Tyrone, used his free hand to open the passenger door and yank Willie out of the car. Both Bell brothers were surprisingly light-weight despite their sinewy physiques. He then conducted a one-handed search of Willie's body but came up empty."

"Open the trunk," Eli ordered Willie, shoving both brothers toward the rear of the car.

"Fine." Willie stumbled, but then righted himself. He released the button and opened the trunk. "You ain't gonna find nothing in there."

"I didn't expect to." He glanced down into the immaculate trunk. "You're too smart to stash the good stuff in your trunk. I better not catch you dealing out of your mama's house."

Willie stiffened. "That sounds like a threat to me."

"Because it is." Eli slammed the trunk shut. "Flora doesn't need your kind of trouble. Neither does Thea."

"Shut up, man," Tyrone said, kicking the gravel at his feet. "You don't know nothing about my mama or my baby sister."

Eli squared his shoulders. "I know more about your family than you think," he said, staring him down. "Flora and I have been friends for years. She's told me all about the heartache you've brought her. She deserves better. And so does Thea. Your sister seems like a sweet girl. Have you ever considered what kind of example you're setting for her? She doesn't stand a chance growing up in the shadow of brothers like you."

"Mind your own business, pig." Tyrone puffed out his chest. "We take care of our folks and you take care of yours. That Annie now. She's a hot little piece of ass. How's she kin to you? She your niece or something? I wouldn't mind dipping my wick in her—"

Eli whipped his pistol out of his holster and held it under Tyrone's chin. "Say another word about Annie and I'll put a bullet in your brain. Is that understood?"

Tyrone nodded, his nostrils flaring.

"All right, then," Eli said, returning his revolver to his holster as a passing car drew near. "Let's all take a deep breath and calm down." He knew his charges against the Bell brothers wouldn't stick. No good would come from locking them up for twenty-four hours. He needed them on the streets where they could get into trouble. And when they did he'd be standing by to catch them. He uncuffed Tyrone and handed him back his switchblade. "I'm willing to forget about this little exchange. At least for now. Thea and Annie are friends. Arguing won't help either of our families."

Eli had lost count of the number of years since he'd last had a drink. He seldom experienced the craving anymore, but his confrontation with the Bell brothers had unnerved him to the point his hands trembled. He and Sam, both recovering alcoholics, refused to keep booze in the house for exactly this reason, for weak moments of temptation like these. Needing fresh air, he changed into jeans and a flannel shirt and went out to the back patio to fire up his Big Green Egg.

Sam found him there twenty minutes later, staring into the blazing fire. "I thought the point of the Egg was to slow-cook the meat."

"Huh?" His head shot up. "Did you say something?"

"Isn't the point of the Egg to slow-cook the meat?" She gestured at the grill, at the flames licking out at him. "We can roast hot dogs and marshmallows over that bonfire."

"Oh! Sorry." He lowered the heavy ceramic lid. "I had my mind on something else."

"Clearly." Sam massaged his back. "Want to talk about it?"

"I was just thinking about Annie. The poor kid has so much on her plate. She really needs a friend right now, and I'm glad she has Thea to talk to, but I don't think the Bell home is a safe place for Annie to visit. Not with Thea's derelict brothers hanging around. Not after what happened today."

"That doesn't sound good." Sam rested her chin on his shoulder. "What happened today?"

"I pulled the brothers over for running a red light. The oldest boy, Tyrone, was driving. He tried to bribe his way out of a ticket. We had a heated exchange. And I'm worried they'll take out their anger at me on Annie."

"I see. We better sit down." They moved to the wicker love seat. "Start at the beginning and tell me everything."

Eli described in detail not only the red light incident from that afternoon but also the scene in from of the Minute Mart late last week when Tyrone hassled the innocent young woman.

"Sounds like things are pretty hostile between you two," Sam said.

"That's an understatement." He leaned against Sam for

comfort. "Things might get worse before they get better. I'm on a mission to get the two of them off the streets for good."

Sam turned to him and took his face in her hands. "You be careful, Eli. If those boys are as dangerous as you say they are, your life could be in jeopardy too. As for Annie . . ." Her hands slid down his cheeks and rested on his shoulders. "I'm not even sure if she's ever been to Thea's house. I'll explain the situation to Faith and she can talk to Annie. If I know Faith, she's already on top of the situation. Remember she was in the emergency room the other night when we met Thea. She heard the exchange between the two of you. She knows the Bell brothers are dangerous. I'm sure she's looking for a concrete reason to keep Annie away from their house."

"Tell Faith to blame it on me when she talks to Annie. Anything to keep her safe from Thea's brothers. I'm telling you, they are no good." He buried his face in his hands. "The way they talk about Annie makes me sick to my stomach."

Sam brought his head to her breast. "Let's try not to think about it anymore," she said, stroking his hair. "If the grill is ready, I'll bring out the ribs. Then I can tell you about my dilemma."

Lifting his head, he stared into her deep blue eyes. The compassion and understanding he found there made everything right again. "That sounds like a good plan." He kissed her softly on the lips. "Happy Valentine's Day. We haven't been married long, but having you around makes my world a better place. I think I'll keep you."

"Good!" She bit his lip playfully. "Because I'm not going anywhere."

He stood and pulled her to her feet. "Except inside to get the ribs. We should have put them on the grill a half hour ago."

"They're ready to go. They've been marinating in rub all day." Sam disappeared inside and returned a minute later with the ribs.

"Great goodness!" Eli said when he saw the platter piled high with four racks of ribs. "Who'd you invite to dinner, the whole USC football team?"

"You know how my family loves ribs. But to answer your question, it's mostly the adults tonight—Mom, Bill and Jackie, Faith and Mike. Plus Bitsy of course. The teenagers are tied up with projects and homework."

Together they forked the ribs on the Egg. Eli closed the lid and manipulated the draft door at the bottom and the metal wheel on top until the Egg reached his desired temperature. They returned to the love seat. "We're lucky. It's a perfect night for grilling. I'm glad the sleet storm on Sunday was short-lived."

"Typical Carolina weather. Blink hard and it will change." She looped her arm through his, nestling up to him. "Did you get me a present for Valentines Day? Because I got something for you. But you can't have it until after everyone leaves tonight."

"Now *that* sounds interesting. I have something for you as well. And you're gonna model it for me later." Eli could hardly wait to see her in the sexy teddy he'd bought.

Sam ran her tongue up his neck to his ear. "Should we call them all now and tell them not to come?" she whispered, her voice husky with desire.

"Nope. I'm sorry but you'll have to wait. We promised them dinner. And dinner we shall deliver." He kissed the top of her head. "Besides, the anticipation will make your pleasure more intense."

"You think so, do you?"

"I know so." He settled back against the cushions. "Now tell me about your dilemma."

"Well . . ." She tucked one leg beneath her. "Heidi is thinking about opening a gourmet shop in Charleston, and I'm considering investing in it."

"A gourmet shop? I thought Heidi was a wedding planner."

"She caters events, including but not limited to weddings. The converted warehouse she's looking at has a commercial kitchen in the back. She's planning to operate her catering business from there. She would sell specialty items, entertainment goods, and prepared foods in the shop out front like we do at Sweeney's."

"You mean she'd be competing with Sweeney's?"

Sam smacked him on the chest. "Don't be ridiculous. You really know nothing about retail. Charleston is forty minutes away, a different city entirely. And she would not limit her provisions to seafood."

"Did she come to you asking for money?"

"Not at all. I volunteered. We talked about it last week, when I saw her at the hospital during Annie's surgery. Heidi took a second look at the warehouse today and sent me some pictures. Here." She handed him her phone.

He swiped through the pictures. "I'm impressed. The place looks like it has real potential." He handed her back the phone and added, "Careful. You might find yourself commuting to Charleston like Jackie."

"I don't think that's the kind of partner Heidi is looking for. But I might have to make a day trip to Charleston every now and then. Would that bother you?"

He draped his arm around her waist and drew her close. "Not at all, sweetheart. I'm excited for you. If this is something you really want to do, I'll support you in every way."

SIXTEEN

FAITH

Faith left the others in the kitchen to finish preparing for dinner, and wandered back to Sam's so-called living room, which was less formal and more an upscale family room conducive to lounging fireside and watching television. Standing at the bank of windows, she watched the pink sun disappear over the horizon at water's edge. Faith's porch, four houses down, offered the same view, but somehow the sunset from her sister's charming bungalow was different. Sam and Eli's stylish retreat away from the world. Their love shack. Faith admired what Sam and Jackie had done to the place. The neutral shades, more taupe than gray. Sofas covered in velvet and wool rugs in geometric patterns. Elements of wood and glass with accents in shades of cool blues that extended the indoors to the waterfront beyond the wall of windows.

Faith couldn't imagine this decor in her home, not with a puppy's muddy paws and a seven-year-old's peanut butter fingers. Another baby would add highchairs and playpens and a host of other gadgets to the mix. Another baby would make her that much further removed from becoming an empty nester like Sam was now and Jackie would be in six months. She didn't begrudge

Sam her happily ever after. Her sister had devoted her life to her family and raised her son on her own for twenty years. She deserved to have the love of her life and her dream house on the water.

Faith and Mike would have their own couple's paradise one day. Sooner rather than later if they didn't adopt another baby. Every year, Bitsy became more independent. She'd be babysitting for the neighborhood children before long. Then driving. Then going to proms. Then applying to colleges. Why didn't the idea of having more time to herself and more time alone with Mike seem more appealing? Because, if given the option, she'd rather fill her home with the sound of ten children's laughter.

Moving across the room to the sitting area, she slipped off her ballet flats and curled up in the corner of the plush sofa, enjoying the crackling and popping of the fire while she sipped her champagne. To christen the new room and celebrate the day of love, Jackie had brought over two bottles, one alcoholic and one nonalcoholic. The bubbles tickled Faith's nose and made her head feel fuzzy.

Sam had told Faith about Eli's encounter with Thea's brothers earlier that day. Faith was irritated with Eli for provoking the Bell boys, but, at the same time, she felt relieved. He had given her the excuse she needed to forbid Annie from visiting Thea's home. A parent, biological or otherwise, was always in a position to forbid their child from doing something, but preventing that child from actually doing it, especially if they were determined to do it, was another matter entirely. Faith knew little about Annie's relationship with Thea. She'd never known the girl existed until Thea appeared in the emergency room at the hospital the night of Annie's accident. Maybe Faith was worrying about something she didn't need to worry about. When she got home tonight, she would casually mention to Annie about Eli's run-in with Thea's brothers and suggest that the Bell home might not be the safest place for her to spend time.

Faith thought back to the conversation she'd had with Mike the night before, during the early hours of the morning when they'd both been unable to sleep from worrying about Annie. She had argued, "We can't let her have an abortion, Mike. It's just not right."

"I don't know how you plan to stop her," Mike said, staring up at the ceiling, one arm propped behind his head. "We've tried talking to her. She appears to have made up her mind."

"She's still vulnerable from the accident. She needs more time to think things through. She can't have an abortion without parental consent, anyway."

"You're forgetting that Annie has three parents. Do you really want her running to Heidi for help?"

"She wouldn't do that. Heidi is not on her favorites list at the moment."

"Maybe. Or maybe not. People take drastic measures when they're desperate. Especially teenagers." He rolled over to face Faith. "Listen, honey," he said, fingering a strand of hair off her forehead. "As her legal guardian, I'm not gung ho about Annie terminating her pregnancy. But as a doctor, I feel she has the right to make her own decisions about her body. She's an astute young woman. I trust her judgment. If she's determined to terminate the pregnancy, I will find the right clinic and take her there myself. I'll insist she talk to Cooper first beforehand. That goes without saying. But I'm convinced we'll lose Annie if we don't support whatever decision she makes."

Placing her back to him, Faith moved in close, letting him spoon her from behind. "We've already lost her. She just hasn't left the nest yet."

"There comes a point in life when all parents lose their children. At least the children as we know them. We can't stop them from growing up. But the role we get to play in their future depends on how we handle them during these volatile years. If we treat them with the respect they deserve and offer guidance when they ask for it, we can transition our relationships from one of authority to one of friendship." Mike blew in her ear. "And that, my lovely wife, means we get to babysit our grandchildren whenever we want."

---

"There you are, Mama. I've been looking all over for you." Bitsy climbed onto the couch and snuggled in close to Faith. "I made this for you." She handed her a heart fashioned out of pink construction paper. "Happy Valentine's Day."

Faith kissed the top of her head. "And Happy Valentine's Day to you too, my little lovely. I will keep this in my special Bitsy folder. When I look at it, I'll think of you just as you are right now, with chocolate all over your lips."

"Oops." Bitsy's tiny fingers covered her mouth. "Sam made chocolate-covered strawberries for dessert. Mike said I could have just one." She held up her pointer finger to demonstrate.

"Well . . . okay." Faith lifted her eyes to the ceiling, pretending to be upset. "Since it's Valentine's Day, and you only had one, I guess it's okay. Just this once."

"But I can have more for dessert, right?" Bitsy asked and stuck her tongue way out to lick her lips.

"As long as you eat your dinner. Speaking of which. What's going on in the kitchen? Is the food almost ready? My tummy is hungry for Eli's barbecue ribs."

"Mine too! Aunt Sam said that dinner will be ready soon." Bitsy tilted her head back and looked at Faith upside down. "Mama, where do babies come from?"

Faith touched her daughter's nose. "They come from God. You learned that in Sunday school."

"Does the daddy help put the baby in the mama's tummy?"

"It's a complicated process but, in a nutshell, that's exactly what happens. I'll explain it to you when you're a little older."

Faith lifted her daughter up off the sofa. "Come on. Let's go see if we can help make dinner ready sooner."

Ten minutes later, all eight family members gathered around Sam's new heart pine farm table. Eli said the blessing and they all dug in. Smacking lips and licking fingers, they polished off four racks of ribs, a large bowl of Caesar salad, and a platter of twice-baked potatoes. The conversation was relaxed as everyone shared events from their lives since they were last together on Christmas Eve.

Faith's mother was wiping barbecue sauce off Bitsy's face with a wet wipe when the child blurted, "Guess what, Lovie? Cooper helped God put a baby in Annie's tummy."

Faith froze with a forkful of baked potato poised in midair. Silence fell over the room as seven sets of eyes darted around the table. Faith set her fork down.

"Oh really?" Lovie said, clearing her throat. "Isn't that interesting." She rose from her chair and took her granddaughter by the hand. "Why don't you and I go into the kitchen and cut that yummy lemon chess pie Sam brought home from the market?"

"But I want more chocolate-covered strawberries too," Bitsy said, skipping alongside her grandmother.

"You can have both, my sweet little granddaughter," Lovie said, swinging her arm in rhythm with Bitsy's.

The awkward silence remained until Lovie and Bitsy had left the room. "Is this true?" Jackie asked, her hazel eyes radiating fury.

Faith wiped her mouth and returned her napkin to her lap. "I'm afraid so."

Jackie reached for her glass and drained the rest of her champagne. "And just when were you planning to tell me about this development?"

Mike placed his arm around the back of Faith's chair. "We only just learned about it ourselves."

"Does Cooper know?" Bill asked.

"Not yet," Mike said. "At least not that we're aware of."

"Cooper broke up with Annie right after the accident, while she was still in the hospital," Faith explained. "Which makes things a little awkward for Annie. As you can imagine, she's quite upset."

"Upset!" Jackie leapt to her feet. "She damn well better be upset. She just ruined both their lives." Turning her back on them, she stalked to the window. "This is a parent's worst nightmare come true. Seriously, Faith. I specifically remember us talking about this at Christmas. How could you let this happen?"

Faith inhaled deeply, steadying her breath. "I could say the same thing to you," she said to Jackie's back. "Why was Cooper not carrying a condom in his wallet? Why did you leave your house unchaperoned on New Year's Eve when both your teenage sons have girlfriends? But casting blame will not solve this problem. We need to rally behind our kids, to help them make the right decision about the baby."

Jackie spun around on her heels. "And what is the right decision about the baby, Faith? Sounds to me like you've already made it for them."

"Nothing has been decided for sure," Faith said. "For the record, I think it would be a mistake for Annie to have an . . . to terminate the pregnancy. But my opinion isn't the one that matters."

"Neither is mine. But, *for the record*, I don't think they should consider getting married and raising this child on their own. I'm not ready to be a grandmother anymore than my son is ready to be a father. They have their whole lives ahead of them."

Bill stood up from the table to face his wife. "Let's go home. We're not going to settle this matter tonight. Not here, in front of your family."

"I agree." Jackie snatched up her bag from a nearby chair. "We need to break the news to Cooper and hear his side of the story before we decide our next move."

"If you'll excuse us," Bill said to the table. "You can under-stand this has come as a shock to us. We'll be in touch when we're ready to discuss the matter." They retrieved their coats from the closet in the foyer and disappeared out the front door.

"That went well," Sam said once they were gone.

"It could've been worse." Eli tossed his wadded-up napkin on his plate. "Imagine if Bill hadn't been here."

A series of moans and groans circled the table.

Mike tipped his head in the direction of the kitchen. "What I want to know is, how did *she* find out about the baby?"

"She overheard Sam and me talking to Annie on Sunday." Faith elbowed Mike. "When *you* were supposed to be keeping her occupied."

Mike's face turned as red as the centerpiece, a bouquet of roses that Eli had brought home to Sam.

"If you ask me, we got off easy tonight," Sam said. "But we need to prepare ourselves for the wrath of Jackie yet to come."

## SEVENTEEN

ANNIE

Annie was doing her homework at the kitchen table, with her books spread out in front of her and Snowflake asleep at her feet, when the others arrived home from dinner at Sam's. Instead of the usual thirty-minute story time, Faith and Mike put Bitsy straight to bed. With solemn expressions, they joined her, taking seats on the opposite side of the table as though preparing to interview her for a job position.

"Uh-oh. What's wrong?" Annie asked, looking from one to the other.

Faith placed her hands on the table, fingers splayed. "Remember the other day when we were in the living room with Sam, when you broke the news to us about being pregnant?"

Annie nodded. "Why?"

"Bitsy overheard us talking. She blurted out about the baby at dinner tonight."

Annie's stomach turned sour and bile rose in her throat. "Are you serious?"

"Unfortunately, yes," Mike said. "I'm so sorry, honey."

She cupped her good hand over her mouth. "Oh shit. Was everyone there?"

"All the adults including Lovie," Faith said as though reading Annie's mind. "She handled it well. She's been through it before with Sam."

Annie tossed her pen down on the table. "That's different, don't you think? Sam was thirty years old and engaged to be married to Jamie's father at the time."

"My mother loves you, Annie. She's doesn't cast judgment on others. Except on her three daughters." Faith offered her a weak smile.

Annie spoke out loud as she considered the implications of Faith's news. "Thank goodness Cooper wasn't there. But Jackie was, so I'm guessing he knows by now. Did she go ballistic?"

"Having Bill there helped temper the situation," Mike said. "He hurried Jackie out the door before she exploded."

Annie turned away from them, staring out the window into the dark night. "I should thank Bitsy. She did me a favor. At least I don't have to be the one to tell Cooper that I'm pregnant."

"We'll give everyone a few days to settle down before we proceed to the next step," Mike said.

"I guess that next step is me talking to Cooper." Annie dreaded the confrontation. She envisioned his face, full of pity. Or would it be anger? She was never sure of his emotions anymore.

Mike reached for Annie's good hand. "We understand if you don't want to talk to him alone. Either or both of us are more than willing to be there with you."

"Cooper will agree to terminate the pregnancy. I'm not worried about that. He is all about leaving for college with no strings attached." Annie spun her laptop around and slid it across the table to Mike. "I was researching the procedure when you came in. Too bad the baby granny can't sign the consent forms. I'm sure Jackie will be eager to get rid of the fetus. Oops, my bad. It's still considered an embryo until eight weeks after conception."

Annie saw Faith cringe, the reaction she'd sought. She hated being such a bitch to her when all Faith had ever been was kind, but she didn't understand why Faith was being so stubborn. Terminating the pregnancy was what Annie wanted and the best solution for everyone. Get rid of the unwanted pregnancy. Poof, problem solved.

"Annie, please," Faith said. "Do you have to be so graphic?"

"All I need is one parent, grandparent, or guardian to sign," Annie said. "But Lovie isn't my biological grandmother, and my guardians don't support my decision. And since I'm not quite desperate enough to go to Heidi yet, looks like I'm stuck having this baby."

Mike closed the computer. "We'll figure something out, sweetheart. We will support you, whichever way you decide. We just want to make certain you give all your options ample consideration first."

Annie's gaze fell on Faith. "Do you feel the same way?"

"I'm not going to lie. I would prefer you have the baby. Even if that means putting it up for adoption. I'm worried you'll regret it down the road if you have an abortion."

"By down the road, do you mean when I'm living my dream life and studying culinary arts in Italy?"

Faith placed her elbows on the table and clasped her hands. "You can still have your dream career if you put the baby up for adoption. You'll easily be able to hide your pregnancy until the end of the school year. Then, I can homeschool you next fall until after the baby comes."

"Actually, I'm thinking about skipping my last year of high school and getting my GED, regardless of what I decide about the baby. I want to study food, not British literature and US history." Annie gestured at the books on the table in front of her. "You think I haven't thought this thing through, but I have. I know myself. I will have a hard time giving this baby up if I carry it to term. Being a single mother at age seventeen is not what I want from life. I know that sounds selfish, but—"

"All I ask is that you take a few more days to think about it," Faith said. "Please."

"That's asking a lot, Faith." Annie picked up her pen and began doodling little hearts on her notebook. She felt their eyes on her, willing her to agree to their plea. "Okay, fine," she said at last. "I'll give it until the weekend. I need to talk to Cooper anyway."

"Good." Mike fell back in his chair. "That's settled, then. At least for now." He eyed her books. "I'm glad to see you're getting caught up on your work. I assume that means you're feeling better. How's your pain?"

"Manageable with ibuprofen. I'm going back to school tomorrow. Can one of you give me a ride or should I ask Thea to swing by and pick me up?"

When Faith and Mike exchanged a look of concern, Annie asked, "What now?"

"Eli pulled Thea's brothers over for some type of moving violation today," Mike explained. "He exchanged unpleasant words with them during the encounter. I'm telling you this to make you aware of the situation. Not to scare you. One of Thea's brothers said something derogatory about you. Eli doesn't think, and Faith and I agree, that Thea's home is a safe place for you to be."

Goose pimples broke out on Annie's skin. "What could they possibly say about me? I've never even met Thea's brothers. And I've never been to her house either."

Faith shrugged. "I don't know what they said. Sam didn't elaborate"

"I want you to understand, Annie, that we don't have a problem with Thea," Mike said. "She seems like a nice girl. But her brothers are trouble, based on everything we've heard from Eli. He's had several run-ins with them over the years."

"Okay, I get it. Stay away from the only friend I have." Annie gathered up her books, tucking them under her good arm. "I thought I liked this town. Turns out it's just as bad as everywhere else I've ever lived."

## EIGHTEEN

## COOPER

Cooper's parents pulled into the driveway in his father's Mercedes only seconds after he arrived home from the library. From the pinched expression on their faces, he could tell something was wrong. He grabbed his backpack and got out of the car. "How was dinner?" he asked.

"Lovely." Jackie flung her cape around her body. "Until Bitsy dropped her little bomb and brought the party to a screeching halt," she said, and marched toward the house.

"What bomb?" Cooper asked his father.

His father placed a hand on Cooper's neck and walked him to the door. "We need to talk. It's cold out here. Let's go inside by the fire."

They found Jackie in the kitchen gulping down a glass of wine. "Geez, Mom, slow down. What could a seven-year-old possibly say to upset you so much?"

Jackie slammed her glass down on the counter. "She didn't just say it to me. She announced it to the whole table. Annie is pregnant."

Cooper's jaw hit the hardwood floor. "That's not possible."

Jackie stared him down. "Are you saying it's not your child?"

"That's not what I'm saying." He collapsed against the counter as the events of New Year's Eve rushed back to him. "I'm surprised is all. We had sex only one time, and it didn't go very well."

"Puh-lease!" Jackie's hand shot up. "Too much information." She snatched up her wine glass and took it to the adjoining family room.

Cooper trailed his mother with body slumped and head lowered. Bill poured a Maker's Mark, neat, and joined them.

"You've disgraced this family," Jackie wailed. "I will never be able to show my face in town again."

"Please, Jack. Dispense with the theatrics." Bill took his wife by the hand and led her to the sofa. "Let's all sit down and talk about this situation rationally."

Cooper dropped to the chair, like a bird stunned after flying into a window. *Poor Annie. First the accident. Now this.* "Annie must be devastated."

Jackie snorted, an unbecoming habit she reserved for when she was really angry. "This affects your life too. If she gets some crazy notion in her head about keeping this baby, she will try to force you into marriage. And you can kiss medical school goodbye."

Cooper combed his hands through his auburn mop. "I don't want to be a doctor, Mom. But that's a subject for another day."

Bill's eyebrows danced across his face. "That's news to me. You've wanted to be a doctor since you were a boy."

"No, Dad. *You* wanted me to be a doctor. I went along with it to make you happy. I've decided to major in graphic design."

"Graphic design?" Jackie said as though the words tasted sour in her mouth. "That sounds more like a hobby than a career."

"This might come as a surprise to you, but success isn't defined by medical and law degrees."

Bill leaned forward, placing his elbows on his knees. "Let's not get sidetracked here. We can discuss Coop's career choices some other time. For now, we need to focus on the crisis du jour."

She snorted again. "He won't have any career choices if Annie has her way. He may very well end up working at Sweeney's for the rest of his life."

"Chill out, Mom. Obviously, getting married wouldn't be my first choice, but Annie didn't get into this situation alone. I'm just as much to blame as she is. Maybe even more so."

"I won't argue with you there," Bill said. "After all the conversations I've had with you boys about practicing safe sex. I even bought you a box of condoms. Why didn't you use one?"

Cooper thought about the box of Trojans his father had given him when he turned sixteen. On a boring Saturday night last winter, he and Sean had blown their condoms up like balloons and stuffed them in a friend's car while the friend was out on a first date with the hottest girl in their grade.

"Because I'm not experienced at these things. And I didn't think to use one. It all happened so fast. So see, I'm more to blame than Annie. I should have been looking out for her. I should have protected her."

Jackie let out an exaggerated sigh. "Your careless behavior may have cost you your future."

"Why are you so sure Annie wants to keep the baby? Did she say that?"

"I haven't talked to Annie, but I know girls like her. She'll try to sink her claws into you any way she can. She had her eyes set on you from the beginning. My guess is, she's been planning this for months."

Cooper's face turned a shade of red a little less orange than his hair. "Shut up, Mom. You don't know what you're talking about."

Jackie stood suddenly. "Like hell I don't. And don't you ever tell me to shut up again."

"You need to calm down, Jackie. And you, son, need to watch your mouth," Bill said, glaring at each of them in turn.

Cooper looked away. "Sorry, Dad." He removed his cell phone from his pocket.

His mother loomed over him. "Who are you calling?"

"Who do you think? I'm calling Annie. She must be going out of her mind."

"Oh no you don't." Jackie seized the phone and tossed it onto the carpet across the room. "I forbid you to communicate with anyone in this family unless one of us is present." She gestured in her husband's direction.

Cooper rolled his eyes. "That's ridiculous. Why?"

"Because Annie may be planning to file a paternity suit. And we don't want you to say anything that might implicate yourself."

Cooper appeared dumbfounded. "Why would she need to file a lawsuit? The paternity isn't in question. I admit to being the father."

Bill interlaced his fingers. "I have to agree with your mother this time, son. We should proceed with caution. When you speak to Annie, you need someone present who can be objective, not just about what's best for her but about what's best for you. After a couple of days, when we've all had a chance to think the situation through, we will sit down together with Faith, Mike, and Annie."

"I have meetings in Charleston tomorrow and Thursday that I can't put off," Jackie said. "The three of us will talk more about this when I get home on Friday. When we've decided our position, we will schedule a time to meet with Faith, Mike, and Annie over the weekend."

"You're crazy!" Cooper jumped up out of the chair. "I can't wait until the weekend to talk to Annie. This is just as much my problem as hers. She needs to know she's not alone in this." Cooper made a move toward his cell phone, but his mother beat him to it.

She slipped the phone into the pocket of her silk tunic. "You can have it back in the morning." She kissed her fingertips and touched his cheek. "I'm sorry, sweetheart. I'm merely looking out for your best interests."

———————

Cooper never promised his parents he wouldn't talk to Annie. He thought it absurd for them to ask him to avoid her, especially since they attended the same school. But his parents were so pissed off, he figured he'd better try. Shouldn't be that hard. He didn't share any classes with Annie. He passed her in the hallway several times during the day, but they no longer ate lunch at the same table in the cafeteria. On this particular Wednesday, however, he couldn't get away from her. He saw her in the parking lot before school. Sat behind her at morning assembly. And encountered her in the library after lunch for the bimonthly lockdown drill. Each time her eyes searched his for answers. Each time he forced himself to look away. Lucky for him, fate took control of the situation when he requested a hall pass to use the restroom during last period and collided with her as she was exiting the women's room.

"Annie . . . I . . .uh . . . I don't really know what to say."

"Then don't say anything, Cooper. I get it. You've been avoiding me all day. You've made it obvious how you feel. You didn't want to be with me *before*. I'm sure you don't want to have anything to do with me now that I'm pregnant."

She started to walk off and he grabbed her good elbow. "I would have called last night when I heard the news, but my mom took my phone away from me."

"Why'd she take your phone away?" Annie's Bambi eyes grew wide. "You mean, so you couldn't call me? Wow! I knew she'd be upset, but I didn't think she'd go that far."

"I haven't seen this uber-bitch side of Mom in a while. You've gotta understand, though, we just learned about the situation last night. My parents need time to wrap their minds around the problem. They asked me not to talk to you until we can all sit down together."

Annie yanked her arm away. "No amount of time is going to make this *situation* any easier for your mother. Tell them they don't need to get involved. I can handle it on my own."

He slumped back against the wall and pulled her gently with him. "You shouldn't have to handle it alone, Annie." He wrapped his arms around her and kissed her hair. "This is just as much my problem as it is yours. I care about you. My feelings for you haven't changed."

Annie sniffled. "Then why did you break up with me?"

"Because I needed to figure out my life. But all that seems so far away now. I will stick by you no matter what you decide. If you want to get married and have this baby, then that's what we'll do. Accident or not, we've created a human being that is part me and part you. I have to say though, if it's a girl, for her sake, I hope she gets your hair and not mine."

Annie pushed away from him. "I like your hair." She ran her hand across the top of his head. "I have to say I'm surprised. I thought you'd be more upset."

"I *am* upset. Of course I'm upset. But we made a reckless mistake. I'm trying to handle it like an adult."

"I don't want to mess up your life, Cooper, anymore than I want to mess up mine. I don't think either of us is ready for marriage and a family."

"Are you saying you want to—"

She pushed off the wall. "Get the hell out of this town as soon as I can? Yes, that's exactly what I'm saying." Staring down at the ground, Annie shifted her weight from one foot to the other. "I don't want to have this baby, Cooper. I want to terminate the pregnancy. Unfortunately, I'm too young to do it on my own. I told Faith and Mike I'd think about it until the weekend.

So that's what I'm doing. They think I'm going to change my mind, and put the baby up for adoption, but I won't. Mike will eventually give in and sign the consent forms. At least I hope so."

A heaviness settled over him. Wasn't an abortion what he wanted? To get rid of the problem so they could all move on with their lives. "I'll go along with you, if that's what you really want. But I think we need to talk about all the options first."

Annie's body went rigid. "I'm so tired of hearing that. Why won't everyone stop talking and start listening?"

## NINETEEN

ANNIE

T hea dropped Annie off at home after school on her way to work at The Grill. She crawled into bed, drew the covers up over her head, and fell fast asleep. The sound of voices in the hallway outside her bedroom woke her an hour later.

Her door flew open and Bitsy skipped into the room, stopping short at the sight of Annie in the bed. When she tiptoed over to her side and saw that Annie's eyes were open, Bitsy asked, "Do you want to take Snowflake and me for a walk?"

"Not today, Bits. I have a lot of homework."

Bitsy's eyes traveled the room, falling on Annie's backpack on the floor beside the door. "Then why aren't you doing it?"

"I was taking a nap. I needed to work up the energy to study."

Bitsy climbed into bed beside Annie. Placing her tiny hand on Annie's tummy, she asked, "Is the baby gonna make you fat?"

"I don't know, squirt. Can we please not talk about it?"

Bitsy cocked her head to the side. "Why not?"

Annie brushed a strand of lank brown hair out of Bitsy's face. "You know how mad it makes you when we're having a family party and all the grown-ups keep telling you it's time to go to bed, but you want them to forget about your bedtime so you can stay up late?"

"Uh-huh."

"Well, that's how I feel. I just want everyone to talk about something else for a change."

"Okay," Bitsy said, even though Annie was pretty sure she didn't understand. The little girl hopped off the bed and started for the door. "I'm gonna get a snack. Do you want one?"

"Sure. I'll have whatever you're having."

Bitsy spun around, her tiny finger pointing at the ceiling. "Don't move! I'll be right back. We can have a tea party in your bed."

Annie settled deeper beneath the covers. She thought back to her encounter with Cooper in the hallway. She could still feel his body against her, hear his voice close to her ear. *My feelings for you haven't changed.* Maybe they could have a future together after all. She closed her eyes and tried to imagine being married to Cooper with their orange-haired little girl or boy playing at their feet. His family had plenty of money to help them. But she didn't want their support. She preferred to make her own way in the world. She'd be stupid to say no if his parents offered for them to live in the guest cottage out at Moss Creek Farm. At least for a while. She could work at Sweeney's while Cooper got his degree. She wondered if the College of Charleston had a graphic design program. Charleston was only forty minutes away. Not such a long commute. Or he could spend the week with his mother at her show house—the current renovation project she never stopped talking about—and come home on the weekends. What was she saying? Love conquers all? Did she and Cooper love each other enough to make a marriage work? He could end up resenting her for trapping him into a marriage and family he wasn't ready for. Or she could end up like her mother, bailing out on Cooper and the baby and running away to culinary school in New York.

*Heidi.* She'd only been a few years older than Annie was now when she got pregnant. She wasn't married to Annie's father at the time. Had she considered terminating the pregnancy, ridding herself of the baby she clearly did not want? She'd only lasted six months before she took off for Hollywood. Had she always aspired to be a movie star? Or had she jumped at any opportunity to get out of a miserable situation? Heidi was pretty now. No doubt she'd been hot back in her prime.

Annie had never asked Heidi about her past. She'd never had the opportunity. Never wanted to know. Until now.

Bitsy appeared in the doorway. "Our snack is ready. But Mama says we have to eat it in the kitchen."

Annie's stomach rumbled and she realized she hadn't eaten since lunch. "What's on the menu?"

"Peanut butter on apple slices and chunks of cheese."

Annie swung her legs over the side of the bed. "Sounds yummy," she lied. It sounded like a snack for a seven-year-old, not a pregnant woman. She was hungry enough to eat a large pepperoni pizza by herself.

Faith was waiting for them at the kitchen table, a glass of sweet tea in front of her. "How was school?" she asked, looking up when they entered the room.

"Fine. I'm pretty much caught up with the work I missed." She pulled out the chair opposite Faith.

"How did you get home?" Faith asked, an accusatory tone in her voice. "Bitsy and I waited for you in the carpool line for thirty minutes."

"Thea gave me a ride. I didn't know you were planning to pick me up. Why didn't you text me?" The image of her cell phone tucked away in the front pocket of her backpack came to mind.

"I tried. You didn't respond." Faith took a sip of tea and set her glass down. "You know how I feel about you hanging out with Thea." Her gaze shifted to Annie's stomach. "You have precious cargo to protect."

"Sorry," Annie said in a petulant tone as the voice in her head screamed, "Everyone please stop talking about this damn baby!"

"Guess what, Annie?" Bitsy said, her mouth gummy with cheese. "Mary picked me for her kickball team today."

"You go, girl!" Annie offered up a high five. Bitsy hero-worshipped Mary—the most popular girl in second grade, with mermaid hair, blue eyes the color of Cookie Monster, and two older sisters who doted on her. "Did you kick a home run?"

"Nope. But I got to first base."

While they devoured their snack, Bitsy babbled on about Mary and the other new friends she was making at school. When Annie first met Bitsy at Faith's wedding back in June, the timid little girl was emerging from twelve months of silence—a post-traumatic stress disorder that had resulted from abuse she'd suffered at the hands of her father. With her mother and new stepfather nurturing her, Bitsy had transformed from a shy child afraid of her own shadow to an outgoing chatterbox.

When she'd finished her snack, Bitsy deposited her plate in the sink, announced that she was going to play with her dolls, and skipped off to her room.

"It's warmer outside than it's been in a while," Faith said. "Would you like to sit on the porch for a few minutes before you start your homework?"

Annie hesitated. "I guess." She retrieved her fleece from her room and went out onto the screened porch. She slipped her good arm in one sleeve, draped the other sleeve over her injured arm, and eased down to the rocking chair beside Faith.

"Still having some pain?" Faith asked, watching her struggle to get comfortable.

"Mostly my ribs."

"Did you see Cooper today?" Faith asked, failing her attempt at nonchalance.

"We talked for a minute in the hallway."

"I assume his parents told him about the baby. What did he have to say?"

"The same as everyone else. He'll support me whatever I decide. Unlike you, he isn't trying to tell me how I should decide."

Faith's head shot up at the anger in Annie's voice. "I think you've misinterpreted my position on the issue. I'm not trying to force you into anything. I'm merely trying to steer you away from having an abortion. If you choose to go full term with the pregnancy, you'll have months to decide what to do about the baby."

Annie lacked the energy to argue with Faith. She stared out over the water, watching the fishing boats returning from a day on the ocean.

"Mike and I have talked a lot about your situation over the past few days," Faith said. "And we agree on all counts. If you keep the baby, we will support you in every way. If you and Cooper decide to get married, you are welcome to live here, although I'm sure Jackie will insist you move into her guest cottage. If you decide to have the baby alone, we will help you raise it. *And,* if you decide to give the baby up for adoption, we'd be honored if you'd consider us as potential candidates to be his or her parents."

Anger pulsed through Annie's body causing her head to throb. "I know you're trying to help, but what you just said is crazy."

"The idea of us adopting the baby might sound unconventional to you, but—"

"Unconventional?" Annie scoffed. "It's a clusterfuck in the making. What happens if I deliver the baby and decide to keep it?"

Faith lifted her hand off the arm of the chair. "Like I said, we'll help you raise it."

"Okay, so what happens if I take a job and move with the baby to California? How will you feel then?"

"I'll miss you like crazy, of course. But I never dreamed you'd make Prospect your home. We're your family, Annie. I'm counting on you to come back and visit for the holidays and summer vacation."

"You say that now, but you'll feel differently when it happens." The kinds of strings she was talking about scared the hell out of Annie. She already owed Faith and Mike so much for taking her in and becoming her legal guardians. If they helped her raise the baby, even for a few years, she'd feel too indebted to them to ever leave.

Faith's head fell back against the rocker. "We have plenty of time to sort through all the details."

Annie jerked her hand away. "I don't know what to think about any of it anymore. I'm so confused with everyone telling me what to do." She stood abruptly, the pain from her broken ribs radiating through her body. "I can't talk about this anymore right now." She stood up and left Faith sitting on the porch alone.

## TWENTY

## HEIDI

Heidi signed her name to the handwritten note, stuffed it in an envelope, and tucked it beneath the ribbon on the brightly wrapped package. She slipped the package in her briefcase satchel and left her apartment to meet Sam.

She and Sam had spoken on the phone several times during the past few days. Much to Heidi's surprise and excitement, Sam conveyed genuine interest in investing in her catering business/gourmet market. In fact, she'd offered an amount that had enabled Heidi to get preapproval from the bank. They were to meet Ken Cook at the warehouse in fifteen minutes for a final walk-through—Sam's first, Heidi's third. If Sam approved of the space and they could agree on some guidelines from which they would operate the business, Heidi hoped to make an offer on the warehouse that afternoon.

Sam was carrying on an animated conversation with Ken in front of the warehouse when she arrived promptly at one o'clock. Heidi slammed the heavy door of her Mustang shut and joined them on the sidewalk. "I see the two of you have already met." She kissed the air beside Sam's cheek and shook Ken's hand.

"We've just discovered we have mutual friends who live in

Prospect," Sam explained. "The Goodman family. Judith Goodman is one of my mother's closest friends. I went to high school with her oldest son, Robert, and Ken went to college with her daughter, Angie."

Heidi smiled. "It's a small world." She gestured at the warehouse's massive front door. "Shall we go inside and take a look around?"

Ken unlocked the door and moved aside so they could enter.

Sam's face lit up as she took in the room. "It reminds me of Sweeney's, only much warmer with the brick walls and oak floors. You could install your coolers over here." She clomped across the room in her cowboy boots. "And set up a table for wine and cheese tastings over here. You could fill the center of the room with fixtures in various sizes–some old and some new—to display your nonperishable food products and fun knickknacks for entertainment. You even have enough room to put in a butcher's counter if you want. Once you get a feel for the neighborhood, you'll have a better understanding of your customers' needs."

Ken stepped forward. "No doubt about it. The space is adaptable for many different purposes. In fact, in the interest of full disclosure, I'm expecting a contract any minute from a young couple who want to open a burger shack."

"Of course you are," Sam said. "You're a realtor. You're required by the code of ethics of your profession to say that every time you show a property regardless of whether it's true."

Sam was teasing, but Heidi saw nothing funny about it. "I'm investing my life savings here, Ken. I will not make an offer until I'm confident this is the right move for me."

"Understood." He headed for the door. "I need to make a phone call. I'll be in my car if you have any questions."

"You were a little hard on him, don't you think?" Sam asked with a chuckle once the door swung shut behind Ken.

"Not at all. He needed to be put in his place. He must think I'm stupid, trying to pressure me into making an offer like that."

Heidi hooked her arm through Sam's. "Come on. Let me show you the kitchen."

Sam circled the entire area, checking out the appliances and the storage closet. "I think it's perfect, Heidi. I can't imagine you'll find a better-suited place."

"I agree." Heidi glanced at her watch. "I don't know about you, but I'm starving. There's a wonderful cafe at the other end of the block. What say we grab some lunch while we work out the few remaining details?"

Over steaming bowls of New England clam chowder, Heidi and Sam discussed the ins and outs of their partnership. They agreed that, for now, Heidi would bear the brunt of the responsibilities, reaching out to Sam when she needed advice. In the future, when and if Annie and Jamie went to work for them, they might consider combining forces.

"Have you given any thought to who you might hire?" Sam asked. "You're gonna need a couple of trusted employees to help manage the business."

Heidi nodded. "I'm thinking of hiring one of my servers to run the kitchen. Lizbeth is graduating from the College of Charleston in May and looking for a full-time job. She's originally from Charleston. Her family lives on the Battery. I'm hoping her connections bring in more catering business. And I have faith in her. She gets the job done, regardless of what the job is."

"She sounds a lot like Annie."

A curious expression crossed Heidi's face. "Now that you mention it, Lizbeth does kinda remind me of Annie." She set her spoon down on her plate. "Speaking of Annie." She removed the package from her satchel on the bench beside her. "Would you mind giving this to her? I would take it to her myself, but I'm trying to respect her wishes by giving her the space she asked for."

Sam took the package. "I'd be happy to." Furrowing her brow, she fingered the pink ribbon on the package. "It's not my place to tell you this. But if I don't tell you, no one else will."

Heidi's body grew rigid. "Tell me what? Is something wrong?"

"I'm afraid so. Annie is pregnant. Cooper is the father, of course."

"Pregnant?" Heidi mouthed the word, but no sound escaped from her lips.

Sam pushed the package aside. "About six weeks along, apparently."

Heidi brought her hand to her mouth. "Oh, my poor baby. I know how she feels."

"Do you, Heidi? Because I remember being pregnant and unmarried like it happened yesterday. The fear and uncertainty about the future. The feeling of being utterly alone in the world. Did you ever consider having an abortion? I know that's a personal question. And I understand if you don't want to answer it."

Heidi's cheeks burned. "I've never told anyone this. And it's a relief to get it off my chest. I would've had an abortion in a second if I'd had the money. How screwed up is that? We couldn't afford an abortion so we got married instead."

"Surely someone would've have loaned you the money."

Heidi looked away. "I'm sure we could've come up with the money. But deep down, I really wanted to keep the baby. I was terrified I'd be a horrible mother. Turns out I was right. Annie is a beautiful person. But not because of anything I did."

"Annie is more like you than you realize."

"That's a nice thing for you to say, even if it isn't true. The reality is I let all three of us down. Annie. Allen. Me."

"There are no instructions for all the challenges that life presents, Heidi. We do the best we can with what we're given."

Sam slurped up several spoonfuls of soup and wiped her mouth. "I'll give Allen credit for raising Annie on his own. I know first-hand how difficult it is for a mother to raise her son alone. But for a father to raise his daughter in the conditions they lived in is almost unimaginable."

Heidi nibbled on a flatbread cracker, not trusting herself to speak. "Does Annie want to have an abortion?"

"She mentioned it on Sunday when she broke the news to Faith and me. But I haven't spoken to her since. I texted her a couple of times, but she hasn't responded. I imagine she's getting hit from all sides."

Heidi pushed her soup bowl away. "Where is Cooper in all this?"

"Honestly, I don't know. I haven't heard anything specifically. But one thing I do know, my nephew is a good kid and he genuinely cares about Annie."

"And Jackie? How is she taking the news?"

"Not well, as you can imagine. I'm not sure I've ever seen my sister so furious." Sam spooned the last of the soup out of her bowl. "And I'm sure we haven't seen the last of it. But Jackie loves Annie. She'll eventually calm down."

"I certainly hope so for the kids' sake." Heidi had worked with the oldest Sweeney sister many times, not only on planning Sam's wedding reception but in arranging events for Jackie's other clients as well. She knew Jackie to be tough but fair. "Annie is lucky to be surrounded by so many people who care about her."

"That's the good news and the bad news," Sam said. "So many people who care about her trying to tell her what to do."

TWENTY-ONE

FAITH

Faith was slipping her coat on, preparing to leave the market on Friday around two o'clock to pick Bitsy up from school, when the back door flung open and Jackie stormed in. "Get Sam. We need to talk." Faith was fairly certain her older sister had never stepped foot in Sweeney's kitchen before, but she marched straight for the business office as though she worked there every day.

Faith stuck her head in the showroom. "Mama," she called. "I need to borrow Sam for a minute. Can you hold down the fort?"

Sam looked up from the slab of tuna she was slicing. "Is something wrong?"

"Jackie's here. She wants to talk to us."

Lovie nudged Sam out of the way. "You go on. I'll finish here."

Sam handed her the knife. "Thanks, Mom. Call me if you get swamped."

Faith heard the gratitude in her sister's voice. They understood how lucky they were that Lovie didn't meddle in their business unless asked.

"Brace yourself," Sam said to Faith in a loud whisper as they entered the office. "This is liable to get ugly."

Jackie's presence sucked all the air out of the tiny office. Sam took a seat behind the desk and Faith opposite her, but Jackie chose to stand.

Towering over them, she said, "Just so you know, I canceled three meetings with potential clients this afternoon. I can't sleep. I can't eat. I'm popping Xanax like breath mints."

"Since when is your anxiety disorder our problem?" Sam asked, leaning back in her chair and propping her boot-clad feet on the desk.

"I don't have an anxiety disorder, thank you very much. I have a prescription for Xanax for emergency use only. And if there was ever an emergency, this is it. We need to resolve this predicament with Annie now, so we can all move on with our lives."

Faith clenched her jaw. "We're talking about a baby here. Not a budget crisis."

Jackie glared at Faith. "I don't need to be reminded of what's at stake. We need to sit down as a family and come up with a solution that works for everyone. But before we do that, I want to make certain the three of us are united." She tapped a red-lacquered fingernail on the desk. "Marriage is off the table. I will not let my son ruin his life because of a stolen moment of passion on New Year's Eve. I don't normally approve of abortion, but in this case I believe it's the best option for everyone involved."

Faith shot up out of her chair. "In other words, you're a hypocrite," she said, particles of spit flying toward her sister. "You're against abortion until it suits your needs."

Sam remained seated. "Shh! Keep your voices down. This is a place of business."

Faith lowered her voice to a near whisper. "I'm against abortion in every circumstance, especially this one. I'm not saying that marriage is the right solution either. Adoption makes the most sense."

Jackie pressed her lips into a thin line. "And let me guess. You and Mike are volunteering to be the adoptive parents."

Faith brought her body up to its full height. "It's an option. Mike and I can provide the child a loving home."

"That's valiant of you. Have you considered all the issues that could arise in the future from such an arrangement? Not just for Annie and Cooper but for the child. When it comes time, how will you explain to the child that his biological parents are really his cousin and his sister?"

Faith dropped her eyes. "I never said it would be easy."

"Y'all are wasting your time arguing about this," Sam said, her palms pressed against the edge of the desk. "We have to respect Annie's wishes. It's her body."

"But she's only sixteen years old," Faith argued. "She needs guidance."

"Of course she needs guidance," Sam agreed. "But she's the most intuitive sixteen-year-old I've ever met. I have the utmost faith in any decision she thinks is best."

"Don't forget about Cooper. He's entitled to a say. No one is going to force my son into marriage." Jackie banged her fist on the desk, causing the cup of ink pens, the computer keyboard, and the stack of plastic invoice trays to vibrate an inch to the left.

Sam rolled her eyes. "Chill out, Jackie. What makes you so sure they are even considering marriage?"

"Because Cooper mentioned it to me last night when I spoke to him on the phone. I specifically told him not to talk to Annie without an adult present. But he went against my wishes. And he offered to marry her. He is under the impression that she's considering it. I'm here to tell you that's not going to happen."

"They could make it work," Sam said. "We would have to help them, of course. But they love each other and—"

"Love each other?!" Jackie's meticulously plucked eyebrows

met her hairline. "If they love each other so much, why did they break up?"

Sam waved her hand in a dismissive gesture. "They're just having a lover's quarrel. I'm not sure what the breakup is about, but it's only a matter of time before they get back together."

Jackie shook her head, her dark hair skimming her shoulders. "You don't know what you're talking about, Samantha. Cooper broke up with Annie because he's getting ready to go off to college and he doesn't want to be tied down to a girlfriend back home. If he feels that way about Annie, who is the love of his life according to you, how's he going to feel about a baby?"

"Annie told me about her conversation with Cooper," Faith said. "She did not mention a marriage proposal. I really don't think marriage is on her mind."

The three sisters began talking at once, their voices escalating in an effort to be heard. When the cacophony reached a near deafening level, Sam clapped her hands loudly. "Quiet!" The room grew silent in an instant. "We are not going to settle anything by arguing. If we cast our votes right now, you are for adoption"—she looked first at Faith and then at Jackie—"and you are for abortion." She aimed her thumb at her chest. "And I vote for Annie keeping the baby. Whether Cooper chooses to be involved or not is up to him. Although I know your son well enough to know he will do the right thing." Sam rose up out of her chair. "The bottom line is, we are not helping that poor girl any by shoving our opinions down her throat. We need to listen to what Annie and Cooper have to say and help them make a decision based on *their* feelings, not ours."

"Fine. Let's just get this thing over with." Jackie swung the door open. "We'll meet at my house tomorrow at three." She exited the office and stomped out the back door without so much as a glance in their direction.

TWENTY-TWO

ELI

Eli's men had the farmhouse surrounded and were awaiting the signal from him before entering. The Bell brothers' Dodge sat in the circular driveway in front of the wide screened porch, giving the appearance that Willie and Tyrone were home alone, despite the dozen or so cars parked haphazardly in the field behind the house.

After his confrontation with Tyrone and Willie on Tuesday, determined to bring them down once and for all, Eli convinced the chief to let him go undercover. He picked up their trail around noon on Wednesday when he spotted the Charger at a pool hall on the south side of town. They led him straight here, to this two-story old farmhouse with a picket fence and a yard full of sprawling oak trees on a country dirt road five miles farther south of the pool hall. A quick search on Google Earth revealed the secondary entrance to the rear of the property from the adjacent wooded lot. The name on the property deed, according to county records, was Romana Peebles. Based on her Facebook profile, she was a stunning Asian woman in her late twenties. Eli assumed Romana was either Tyrone's or Willie's girlfriend.

125

Eli had parked his undercover sedan a quarter mile down the road and for the rest of the afternoon on Wednesday and all day on Thursday, he'd conducted surveillance, hidden in the bushes close to the house. He suspected the Bell brothers were operating a prostitution ring out of the house. Although he had no proof, he expected to find drugs inside the house as well. Mass quantities if his suspicions were accurate.

Eli barked out the command, and his men busted down the front, back, and side doors, entering the house with their weapons drawn. He inhaled a lungful of crisp air, holding it as he listened intently for sounds from inside, praying he didn't hear gunfire. After several excruciatingly long minutes, his friend and sometimes partner, Brad Swanson, reported the all clear.

"You were right, Lieutenant," Brad said over his walkie-talkie. "The Bell boys are operating a regular whorehouse in here. And get this: his customers are upstanding citizens. The country club set. I caught a glimpse of the doctor who repaired my torn ACL several years back."

Eli was not surprised. He'd seen the men who frequented the house. Even recognized a few of them himself. Most were dressed for a day at the office in business attire. The women, however, looked nothing like the fashionable ladies he knew to be their wives.

"I guess they stopped in for a little Friday afternoon delight before going home to spend the weekend with their families. What about Tyrone and Willie? Do you have them in cuffs?"

"I hate to tell you this, Eli. There's no sign of the Bell brothers in here. And aside from several lines of cocaine laid out on a mirror in the drawing room we haven't found any other drugs."

Eli raked his hands through his thick hair. "Keep searching. Their car's out front. They have to be around here somewhere."

"Roger that. What do you want us to do with these . . . um . . . . the occupants of the house?"

"I'll send the paddy wagon around back. Load 'em up and take them to the station. These men have a lot at stake. If they want to keep their extracurricular activities out of the papers, they'll tell us everything we want to know about Willie and Tyrone."

"Ten-four."

Eli called for the paddy wagon and the two K-9 units who were stationed out of sight farther down the dirt road from the house. As they drove up the front driveway, he directed them around to the back and followed them on foot to where chaos awaited. Eli's men led their prisoners out of the house, tugging and pulling on the handcuffs of scantily clad women and businessmen with their trousers wrinkled and the buttons on their crisp white dress shirts mismatched. The women kept their heads lowered, their lips pressed tight and their eyes trained on the ground, while the men complained about the injustice of their arrest. "I'll have your job for this, Lieutenant!" one of the men yelled when he spotted Eli. "Chief Andrews is a personal friend of mine."

"Not for long," Eli hollered back. "Not when he finds out you were here and why."

Eli sent one of the K-9 units on a search of the inside and followed the other around the perimeter of the house. Set free to sniff the backyard, the German shepherd led them straight to a toolshed at the rear of the property. The shed, hidden by overgrown shrubs, hadn't shown up on his Google Earth search. The likelihood that anyone was hiding inside was slim, considering the padlock on the door, but Eli removed his pistol from the holster just in case. He stepped to the side of the door. Speaking softly into his walkie-talkie, he ordered Luke, his most trusted rookie officer, to bring him a crowbar. "Approach with caution," he added.

Luke pried the lock off and kicked the door open. A John Deere mower occupied the majority of the small space. Yard tools

—shovels and rakes and a wheelbarrow with a flat tire—were propped up against the walls on either side.

Eli gave a nod and the K-9 handler allowed his charge to enter. The dog immediately began pawing at the ground beneath the tractor. Eli dropped to his hands and knees and peered under the tractor. "Looks like there's some kind of trapdoor under here." He got back on his feet and checked the ignition for the keys. "Naturally the keys aren't here." He turned to Luke. "Get a crew in here to move this thing out of the way."

Four officers arrived on the scene and helped push the tractor out of the shed. Eli lifted the trapdoor and shined his flashlight inside the dark hole. He climbed down the short ladder and yanked on the chain that controlled the overhead lightbulb. "Bingo."

## TWENTY-THREE

ANNIE

Faith texted Annie during her last period: "*We are meeting at Jackie's tomorrow at three to discuss your situation.*"

Annie: "As if it's anybody's business but mine."

Faith: "You'll feel better once you have a plan. We can talk about it more when I pick you up from school."

Annie: "You don't need to pick me up. I already have a ride."

Faith: "With Thea? I worry about your safety when you're with her."

Annie: "I'll be fine."

Annie caught up with Thea at her locker after school. "Can you give me a ride home before you go to work?"

Thea slammed her locker door shut and hooked her arm through Annie's. "You bet. I don't have to work today."

"You have Friday afternoon off? Woo-hoo!" Annie punched the air. "Let's party. Wanna go get some ice cream? I'm buying. Two scoops of salted caramel on a sugar cone."

Thea laughed. "You're so on."

They were pulling into a parking space at Sandy's Ice Cream Shop on the waterfront when Thea received a call from her mother. Annie's ears perked up when she heard the concern in her friend's voice. "Are you hurt? Do you think you broke anything?" Thea paused, listening. "I'm on my way. Don't try to get up. I'll be there in five minutes." She ended the call and put the car in reverse. "My mom tripped over the rug in the living room. I need to go help her get up."

Annie remembered her promise to Faith and Mike about staying away from the Bell house. But this was an emergency. Surely they would understand. "Should we call 9-1-1?"

"No," Thea said. "This has happened before. You've never met her, but my mom is kinda heavy. Which makes her very clumsy."

They headed north on Creekside Drive. About five miles outside of town, Thea turned left onto a country road. A few small homes dotted the landscape, but most of the area was rural. They drove another half mile before turning down a dirt drive-way. Thea's house was a cinder block box with concrete front steps, but Annie felt right at home when she crossed the threshold into the tiny sitting room.

Thea's mother lay spread-eagled on the floor in front of the sofa, her ample chest rising and falling under labored breathing.

Thea rushed to her side. "How did this happen, Mama? You've got to be more careful."

"Clumsy me. I tripped over my own size tens." Thea's mother zeroed in on Annie. "You must be Annie. You're a pretty little thing, just like Thea described."

Annie's cheeks flushed pink. "Thank you, ma'am." She stretched her good arm out to the woman.

Thea's mother dismissed her with a wave. "You already got one wounded wing, angel. You don't need old Flora breaking your other one."

Flora was far from old. With smooth skin and no evidence of gray hair, Annie figured she was probably in her forties, but her obesity added decades, turning a middle-aged mother into a grandmother.

Thea wrapped her arms around her mother's ample body

from behind and helped her sit up. "Okay, Mama, on a count of three." With a strength Annie didn't know her friend possessed, Thea hauled her mother to her feet. Leaning on her daughter for support, Flora limped back to her recliner in front of the television. Judging from the threadbare upholstery, she spent a good deal of time in that chair.

Flora settled back in the recliner. "Thea, honey, be a good girl and get your mama some juice." She waited for her daughter to leave the room before motioning Annie to the sofa. "Have a seat and visit with me for a while. It's not often I get a chance to talk to someone so young and pretty."

Annie sat down on the sofa at the end closest to Flora.

"I've heard a lot about you, angel. Sounds like you got more than your share of trouble right now."

Annie lifted her gaze. "She told you?" *Does the whole world know I am pregnant?*

"Thea and I have been through a lot together. We learned a long time ago it's best not to keep secrets from one another."

Annie experienced a pang of jealousy. The Sweeney women had been kind and generous to her. She had two substitute aunts, a stand-in mother, and Lovie, who was like the grandmother she'd never known. But it wasn't the same. Annie would give anything to have a real mother. One she could confide in. One who put Annie's needs before her own. One who had nurtured her since birth. One who would never abandon her.

"I've been in your shoes before." Flora glanced down at Annie's black Chuck Taylors. "Mine were never that snazzy. But I know how it feels just the same."

Annie's eyelashes fluttered. "You do?"

"Indeed I do," Flora said, nodding, her dark eyes bulging. "I was younger than you when I got pregnant with my oldest."

"Wow! Considering I'm only sixteen, you must have been pretty young. Did everyone try to tell you what to do?"

"Only my boyfriend at the time. Tyrone's daddy is meaner

than he is. He tried to force me to get an abortion. But I couldn't do it. Everybody's different, angel. There ain't no right or wrong in this situation. Only what's best for you. Listen to your heart and have faith in the Lord, and everything will work out the way it's supposed to."

Thea returned with a tray. She handed each of them a glass of orange juice and passed around a metal tin filled with shortbread biscuits. "Do you mind if we hang out for a few minutes?" she asked Annie, lowering herself to the sofa beside her. "I want to make sure Mama's okay."

Annie knew Faith would be worried about her. As much as Thea was worried about her mother. But they couldn't leave until they were certain Flora was okay. "Of course. I don't have anywhere I need to be."

Flora pointed a shortbread biscuit at her. "You know, Annie, having people telling you what to do means they care about you. They'll support you if you decide to keep the baby. But I'm warning you, raising kids on your own ain't easy. I finally got it right the third time." Flora winked at her daughter. "I don't know what I'd do without my baby girl. Those hellion sons of mine have caused me a lot of pain and heartache. But that doesn't mean I love them any less."

As she sipped her juice and nibbled at her biscuit, Flora talked of her experiences raising three children on her own. Although she never came right out and said it, she hinted that all three of her children had different fathers. They never had enough money for food or clothing, and the boys were always getting into trouble, but there was plenty of love to go around. Much like the way Annie's father had raised her. "You can do anything you set your mind to, angel. But having family around to support you will make it a lot easier."

*Could I do it? Could I keep this baby and raise it on my own?* She loved Cooper. She would never pressure him into marrying her. But he was all about doing the right thing. He would insist on being a part of the baby's life. Having his child would bond them together. Then, maybe one day, when he was ready to settle down . . .

"We're having a family meeting tomorrow to decide my future," Annie said. "I thought I knew what I wanted, but now I'm not so sure."

"From everything you've said and everything I've heard about you and your people, I gotta believe they gonna stick by you. Just don't let them talk you into something you aren't ready for." Flora leaned over the arm of her chair and patted Annie's hand. "You gonna be fine, angel. You're always welcome here, if you ever need to get away."

Annie managed to say thank you despite the lump in her throat. *Damn hormones.*

Thea stood to leave. "I'm gonna run Annie home, Mama. But I'll be right back."

Flora picked up the remote from the coffee table and clicked on the TV. "Take your time, sweet girl. I'm not going anywhere," she said and reclined the chair back as far as it would go.

---

Thea was turning the car around in the yard when a long, sleek BMW sedan whipped in the driveway.

"Who's that?" Annie asked.

The sedan swerved in front of them and skidded to a stop. Thea squinted to see the passengers. "My brothers. But that's not their car."

The driver jumped out of the BMW and strutted across the dirt yard to Annie's side of the car. He tapped on the window and she rolled it down.

"Whose car is that?" Thea asked.

"Nobody you know. Mine's in the shop. Why aren't you at work?"

"I have the afternoon off because they need me for the early morning shift tomorrow. Mama fell again. I think she's all right, but can you stay with her while I take Annie home?"

Thea's brother turned his attention to Annie. "I have a better idea. Why don't you stay here and let me take Annie home?"

The feel of his menacing eyes roaming her body made Annie's skin crawl. She held her breath, praying Thea would decline his offer. She'd rather walk eight miles home than ride in the car with the Bell brothers.

"Thanks anyway," Thea said, "but I'd rather take her myself."

Tyrone fingered a lock of Annie's honey-colored hair. "Why don't we ask Annie who she'd rather ride with?"

Annie shrank as far away from him as she could get without ending up in Thea's lap.

"Are you afraid of me, little girl?"

"I . . . um . . ." Annie lifted her chin. She refused to let this man see her fear. She'd encountered worse—her father's friends who'd shown up at their apartment on the occasional Friday night to play cards and drink whiskey. "No! I'm not afraid of you."

His top lip curled into a smirk. "Good, because I'm not going to hurt you. But I have a message for you to give Eli. Tell him to watch out, because the Bell brothers are coming after him."

## TWENTY-FOUR

## ELI

Eli left the police station and drove straight to the liquor store where he purchased a pint of tequila from a Jose Cuervo display right inside the front door. He wasn't interested in taste. In fact, he had no preference for variety or brand at all. He was solely interested in getting drunk.

The organized chaos at the farmhouse had escalated into complete mayhem at the station. Prospect's small police department was ill equipped to handle the arrest of thirty men and women at once. The fingerprinting, photographing, and confiscation of personal items took the better part of two hours. Chief Andrews became distraught at the sight of so many of the town's upstanding citizens, several of them his golfing buddies, in a holding cell. The chief agreed to drop all charges against the men in exchange for any information they could provide on the Bell brothers. He handled the female prisoners in a different manner. They were prostitutes after all. A weekend in the slammer might teach them a lesson, set them on the path to a better career.

One by one, these gentlemen were led to the interview room. Eli and his coworkers tag-teamed them, berating them for engaging in prostitution, deflating their overgrown egos until they offered up everything they knew about the goings-on at the farmhouse. They spoke of the drug use, mostly cocaine and marijuana, and they described the act of prostitution in more detail than the officers wanted to know. But none of them had any knowledge of the Bell brothers. When shown mug shots of Tyrone and Willie from recent arrests, these upstanding citizens of Prospect denied ever having seen either brother at the farmhouse or around town. In response to these same mug shots, while they also denied having any knowledge of the Bell brothers, the women prisoners' faces turned ashen, their eyelids twitched, and their pulses throbbed at their necks.

"I know you're lying," Eli said, banging his fist down on the table in front of Romana Peebles when it was her turn to be questioned. "Their car has been parked in front of your farmhouse for the past two days. Are you saying you haven't seen them, that Tyrone and Willie Bell aren't your friends?"

She lowered her gaze to the table. "I don't know who you're talking about."

Eli sat down in the chair opposite her. "Ms. Peebles, I don't think you realize exactly what's at stake here. Your name is on the property deed. Which makes you solely responsible for the drugs we confiscated from your toolshed."

She jerked her head up. "What drugs?"

"My men are sorting through them now. But, hidden beneath your riding mower in the toolshed behind the farm, we found several pounds of marijuana, multiple kilos of cocaine, and too many Ziploc bags of pills to count."

A bead of perspiration broke out on her forehead. "I don't know anything about that."

Eli propped his elbows on the table and pressed his fingers together as if he were praying. "The drugs belong to somebody, Ms. Peebles. If not you, then who? Tyrone and Willie? Is one of them your boyfriend?"

Her lip quivered. "Not my boyfriend."

"So he's your pimp?"

Romana gulped in a huge breath of air and sat ramrod straight in her chair. "I told you, Officer, I don't know who you're talking about."

Eli jumped to his feet. "I don't believe this. You claim the drugs don't belong to you, yet you're willing to take the fall for them? You're looking at serious jail time here, Ms. Peebles."

She looked away from him and mumbled, "At least I'll be safe behind bars."

Eli sat on the sofa in a trance, staring at the unopened bottle of tequila on the coffee table in front of him. He didn't hear Sam come in, didn't know she'd arrived home, until she was right in front of him.

"Eli, honey, is everything okay?" She snatched up the bottle, and then let out a sigh of relief when she saw the unbroken seal. "Shall I pour this down the drain?"

"That's not necessary. I'll return it to the store tomorrow and get my money back. The temptation was short-lived. Buying it and bringing it into our house made me feel rotten, like I'd somehow betrayed you."

Sam walked the bottle to the table beside the front door and returned to the sofa. "I take it things didn't go well today." She sat down close beside him.

"We found everything we expected to find and more. Aside from the Bell brothers themselves." He told her about the drugs and the prostitution. "I don't get it, Sammie. Their car was parked in front of the house. We had the place surrounded. I have no idea how they could have gotten away without us seeing them."

"If the house was packed with people," Sam said, "maybe they took someone else's car."

"We thought of that. But, so far, all the other cars are accounted for." He rubbed his eyes with his balled fists. "The chief is irate. After we finished interrogating everyone, he called me into his office and chewed me out. He's giving me the weekend to come up with something concrete against the Bell brothers. If I don't, he's taking me off the case. There goes my promotion. Hell, there goes my future at PPD. I might as well buy a charter fishing boat and cast out my line, because I'm never going to make detective."

"Are you absolutely certain the Bell brothers are involved?"

"I can taste it like I can taste that tequila over there." He dipped his head at the bottle of Jose Cuervo across the room. "Tyrone and Willie Bell are dealing drugs and pimping their prostitutes. Their customers seemed legitimately unaware of their existence, but I'm convinced their whores are hiding something. They're afraid to talk. And they have good reason. Tyrone and Willie will beat them senseless if these women rat them out. The good news, if there is any good news to speak of, is that Romana Peebles will be spending the weekend in jail. Which will give me another chance to talk to her."

Sam massaged his neck. "I know you have a lot going on and I hate to bring this up. But is there any chance Annie might be in danger?"

"Yes. And she is not the only one in danger." Eli placed his arm around Sam and pulled her back against the sofa cushions with him. "I'm worried about you as well. By now, Tyrone and Willie have figured out that I've confiscated their stash. They'll be furious at me for taking away their provisions. They're liable to come after me and the easiest way to get to me is through my family. Because of her relationship with Thea, Annie is an easy target for them."

"I can take care of myself. I have you to protect me." She snuggled closer to him. "It's Annie I'm worried about. She's already dealing with so much. Jackie has called a family meeting for tomorrow at three out at the farm. Can you guess what's on the agenda?"

Eli raised an eyebrow. "Annie's pregnancy?"

"That's right. I guess Jackie has a right, considering the baby is as much her son's as Annie's, but—"

"It hardly seems fair to put Annie in the hot seat."

Sam hung her head. "I feel bad for the poor kid. Cooper broke up with her, and as far as I know, Thea is her only friend. She certainly needs a friend, now more than ever. The last thing I want to do is scare her. At the same time, she needs to be aware of the situation with Thea's brothers."

"I'll call Mike. He'll know how to handle it." Eli gave her a squeeze. "I'm so sorry, honey. The last thing I wanted to do was put my family in danger."

## TWENTY-FIVE

## COOPER

Cooper's mother was pacing the driveway, clicking and clacking in her high-heeled boots behind her SUV, when he returned from his run. Hands on knees, he took big gulps of air until he caught his breath and his heart rate lowered. He straightened to face his mother. "What're you doing out here in the cold? Are you having another hot flash?"

She snorted and crossed her arms. "What do you know about my hot flashes?"

His smiled sparked a mischievous twinkle in his eye. "Dad said that's why your face and neck turn red all the time now."

"I'd appreciate it if you didn't discuss my bodily functions behind my back," she said, drumming her fingers on her arm. "For your information, I was out here waiting for you. We need to talk."

He lifted his shirttail to wipe the sweat from his face. "Can't it wait until after I shower? I'm going to Mark's house to work on a project for my graphic design class."

She cocked an eyebrow. "On a Friday night?"

"I know, right?" He walked toward the house with Jackie hot on his heels. "We're creating some seriously cool vector art."

"I don't understand your sudden fixation on graphics," she said, closing the door behind them.

"It's really no different than your obsession with interior design. I guess I inherited the creative gene from you."

"I would think you'd show a little more concern about Annie's pregnancy and a little less interest in your *vector art*."

"What do you expect me to do, Mom, sit around and sulk all day?" He started up the stairs, but she grabbed a handful of his shirt and held him back.

"Not so fast, mister. I've scheduled a meeting with Annie for tomorrow at three to talk about your situation. I expect you to be here."

"You did what?!" He yanked his shirttail out of her hand.

"You heard me," she said, her jaw set. "We need to come up with a solution that works for everyone."

He stepped back down to floor level. "There's not a solution that will work for everyone, Mom," he said, towering over her. "It's not fair to put Annie on the spot like that. Who all did you invite to this little tea party?"

"Annie, obviously, and my sisters. Their husbands are welcome to come as well. Your father will be here of course."

"Great," he said with an exaggerated eye roll. "Why don't we invite the Prospect High basketball team while we're at it?"

"Watch your tongue, young man." She wagged her finger at him. "I'm not responsible for putting you in this position. But I have every intention of helping you find a solution that won't cost you your future."

Cooper willed himself to calm down. Making his mother angry wouldn't solve the problem. It would only make matters worse. "I understand, Mom. But you said the other night that we would sit down with Annie, Mike, and Faith. What's the point in dragging Sam into it? Annie is going to feel cornered with all of us telling her what to do."

"She happened to be at the market when I stopped by to talk

to Faith. Besides, Annie feels comfortable with Sam." Jackie pointed up the stairs. "Go take your shower. And call Mark. Tell him you'll be late. Your father will be home any minute. We're going to sit down together and decide our position, so we can present a united front tomorrow."

The sudden surge of anger scared him. He'd never experienced those feelings toward his mother. Which was saying something, because she'd pissed him off plenty of times before. He stomped up the stairs before he said or did something he'd regret.

His mother and father were waiting for him on the sofa in the family room, heads close together murmuring to one another, when he came back downstairs. Cooper plopped down in the leather club chair across from his parents. "Can we get this over with? I'm supposed to be somewhere."

Jackie glared at him. "You'll stay here as long as it takes for us to reach a decision we can all live with."

"Honey." Bill rested a hand on Jackie's leg. "Let's not be so hard on the boy. This is a difficult situation for everyone." He turned his attention to Cooper. "Although I agree with your mother that we'll be better off if we're all on the same page. Let's start with you, son. What are your thoughts about a possible solution?"

Cooper shrugged. "It's Annie's body. I'll stand by her no matter what she decides."

"Like hell you—"

Bill shut Jackie up with a warning glare. He leaned forward, clasping his hands in his lap. "You have a lot at stake, Cooper. You can't just let this girl decide your future."

Cooper threw up his hands. "What the *f*. Since when is Annie just some random girl. Everyone in this family worshipped her until this happened."

"You're right," Bill agreed. "We *do* all love Annie. And when the time comes, if the two of you are still together, we will welcome her into our family with open arms. But now is not the right time. You're only seventeen years old."

"I'll be eighteen next week. But I'm pretty sure you already know that."

"The sarcasm isn't helping, son," Bill said.

Cooper hung his head. "Sorry."

"Eighteen is still too young to be a father." Jackie moved to the edge of the sofa. "I'm just going to come right out and say it. Your father and I think Annie should have an abortion." She held her hand up to Cooper before he could protest. "Hear me out. We'll get the best medical care for her. Obviously. We'll even pay for everything. I'll even take her to have the procedure. This way, you and Annie can put all this behind you and move on with your lives."

Bill nodded his agreement. "With no strings attached."

Cooper stared at his parents with his mouth agape. "I can't believe y'all. We're talking about a baby. My baby. A living, breathing, human being."

Jackie lifted her index finger. "Technically, it's not yet a baby. But that's subject to argument. Have you considered how you're going to support this *baby* and its mother? We'll pay for your college. Grad school too, if that's what you decide you want. But we will not pay for you to get married and have a baby."

Cooper jumped up out of his chair, his fists balled at his sides. "Fine! I'll become a fisherman like my grandfather if that's what it takes. You know what? You are both hypocrites." He glared at them in turn. "You taught me to be honorable. You can't pick and choose when to do the right thing. I helped make this mistake. And I have every intention of owning up to it. I never said I wanted to get married. There are options we haven't discussed yet–like adoption. But the right thing for me to do, the honorable thing, is to support Annie in whatever she decides.

This time you don't get to tell me what to do." He spun on his heels and crossed the room in four strides.

"If you leave now, don't bother coming home," Jackie called after him.

He paused in the doorway with his back turned toward her. "This isn't a home," he said. "This is a totalitarian state."

TWENTY-SIX

ANNIE

Annie snatched the phone up from the nightstand when she saw her brother's face light up the screen. She'd been scared out of her mind and worried sick for Eli after her encounter with Thea's brother. She'd changed out of her clothes and crawled into bed as soon as she got home. But she hadn't been able to fall asleep. She couldn't decide what to do about Tyrone's threat. If she confided in Eli, he would insist on telling Faith and Mike. And she would never be allowed out of the house again. At least not with Thea.

She accepted the call. "I trust you've heard my exciting news. Are you ready to be an uncle?"

Jamie had sent her flowers and called her after the accident, but she hadn't wanted to trouble him with her problem of the week. He was already overloaded with schoolwork and baseball practice.

"How can you make jokes at a time like this?" Jamie asked.

"Because if I didn't laugh, I'd go stark raving mad. Like everyone else around here. They're jerking me around, trying to tell me what to do. I'm like their puppet on a string, but now all those strings have gotten tangled into one great big knot. Why won't they listen to what I want, Jamie? I have feelings too, you know."

Jamie sighed. "Of course you do. I'm coming home. I'll help you sort through this mess."

"No!" She sat up in bed. "You can't do that! You have too much work, and the coach will bench you if you miss practice."

"You're more important to me than baseball," Jamie said.

"But you shouldn't have to choose."

Jamie reluctantly agreed to wait as long as she promised to call him if she got in over her head. No sooner had she hung up when the phone rang again.

"I need to see you." Cooper's voice sounded hoarse as though he'd been crying.

"I don't think that's a good idea, Cooper. Besides, I'm already in my pajamas."

"Pajamas? But it's not even seven o'clock. Have you eaten dinner yet?"

"I'm not really hungry," she said, even though she was starving. She and Thea had never made it to Sandy's that afternoon.

"Come on, Annie. You need to eat. Can I tempt you with some ice cream?"

Her stomach rumbled as she weighed his offer against the alternative. Go for salted caramel ice cream or face Mike and Faith in the kitchen. She sighed. "All right. But give me fifteen minutes to change."

When she saw Cooper's headlights in the driveway, she slipped out the front door. She didn't have the energy to face Faith, to answer her countless questions. *Where are you going? When will you be back? Who are you going with? Does this mean you and Cooper are back together?*

She climbed into the Land Cruiser. "What's up?" Noticing his swollen eyes and red nose, she added, "Did something happen?"

"My mother's turned into a pit viper." He put the SUV in

gear and sped off down the driveway. "I can't believe she summoned us for a meeting tomorrow."

Annie gripped the handle on the roof of the SUV when Cooper made a sharp turn onto Creekside. "She wants us to decide what to do about the baby. What's so wrong with that?"

"She doesn't want us to *decide* what to do. She wants to *tell* us what to do."

"Oh." Annie looked away, unable to bear the hurt in his eyes. *I did not inflict this pain on him*, she reminded herself. *This baby, this mistake, is his too.* "I'm almost afraid to ask. What does she want us to do?"

"She wants the problem to go away. She's acting irrational, like a two-year-old who isn't getting her way. She refuses to consider any other possibility. I stormed out of the house, and she told me not to come home. So if I'm not at the family powwow tomorrow, you know why."

Annie bit down on her bottom lip. "I'm sorry, Coop. I never meant to come between you and your parents."

"Hey." He reached over and chucked her chin. "We're in this together. And I've made it clear to them that I'm standing by you."

Having someone share the burden might not be such a bad thing. He was the father after all. "That's just it, though. If we're in this together, I want you to help me decide."

He whipped into the parking lot at Sandy's. He killed the engine and turned to face her. "Okay, then. Two salted caramel cones and one decision coming up."

Annie smiled. "Make mine two scoops, please."

Sandy's was crowded with middle-school kids, but Annie found a table for two near the back while Cooper went to the counter to order. She watched the young girls, their budding breasts and long skinny legs, flirt with the boys their age who had pimples dotting their faces and teeth gleaming with braces. So young with everything ahead of them. Annie thought back to seventh grade when she'd started her period. Because her father had been inept at handling female issues, she'd gone to see the nurse at school who had given her supplies with instructions on how to use them. She still remembered the nurse saying, "You're a woman now. One day you'll be blessed with children. Be careful to protect yourself, so it doesn't happen before you're ready. You can come see me anytime with questions."

*What advice would that nurse give me now?*

Cooper arrived at the table with a cone in each hand. "So, my friend, are we ready to get to work?"

They addressed their dilemma like they would a group project, contemplating at length the implications of every solution.

When Annie mentioned terminating the pregnancy, Cooper said, "You probably don't want to hear this, but I'm flat out against abortion. It's not my body, though, and if that's what you really want, I'll deal with it."

"I have to admit I've been considering it. Because I was scared and it seemed the only way out."

Cooper stuffed the rest of his cone into his mouth and wiped his lips with a napkin. "We can get married if you want, Annie. We'll find a way to make it work. My parents are angry now, but they'll come around. I know they'll help us."

Annie's stomach did a somersault. She loved Cooper. It was easy to imagine their life together. Pushing their baby stroller along the waterfront at sunset. Their toddler running to greet him when he came home from work. In bed together as husband and wife, making love until the wee hours. But even brighter than the vision of them getting married now and raising this baby together loomed the fantasy of her working alongside a great master chef in a five-star restaurant—however selfish that sounded, even to her own ears.

Annie studied Cooper's face for a sign. He was holding his breath. Getting married was not his preferred option. Realizing it wasn't what she wanted either offered her a huge sense of relief. "You can breathe, Cooper. I don't want to get married either." She play-punched him in the arm like she used to do when they were still just friends.

"Are you sure?" His body relaxed, and then stiffened again. "Because if you change your mind, the offer is still on the table."

She reached for his hand and squeezed. "Maybe one day, when we're both living our dreams, we'll find a way to be together. But for now, I'm happy being just friends again. We are friends again, right?"

"Hell yeah!" He punched the air. "And it feels so good. I've really missed you these past few weeks."

Annie choked back tears. "Same." She sat back in her chair. "So . . . by process of elimination, it appears as though we've arrived at adoption. Question is, should we let Faith and Mike adopt the baby or use an agency?"

Cooper frowned. "I'd have to give that some thought, honestly. She's my aunt. It would be kind of weird, watching the kid grow up knowing it's mine. What if, God forbid, he or she ends up with my coloring? I mean, let's face it. My features are pretty distinct. What would we do if the kid figures out you and I are the biological parents? That sounds like a recipe for heartache to me. Especially for Faith and Mike. And what about Bitsy? How would you explain the situation to her? She knows you're pregnant. Asking a seven-year-old kid to comprehend that scenario is asking a lot."

"Faith and Mike are good parents. They'll know how to handle Bitsy if that time comes." Annie fingered the sugar packets in the container in the center of the table. "I plan to leave town after the baby is born, Cooper. I've decided to apply to culinary school." Now that they made the decision to put the baby up for adoption, there was nothing keeping her there. She locked eyes with him. "I won't be coming back to Prospect. Especially if Faith and Mike end up with the baby. It's gonna be really hard for me to give it up after carrying it for nine months. I don't think I'd be able to handle seeing it again."

He ran his finger down her cheek. "So what you're saying is, ten years from now when we're both living our dreams, we'll have to find our way back to one another in New York?"

Annie nodded. "That's where I'll be. Waiting for you.

## TWENTY-SEVEN

## FAITH

Faith dreaded the meeting ahead of her. When Jackie got into one of her moods, she made certain everyone paid. If she was miserable, she wanted everyone else to suffer with her.

As they drove down the tree-lined, cobblestone driveway at Moss Creek Farm, she turned around to face Annie in the back. "Just remember. We don't have to make a decision about anything today."

Annie's smile reached her warm brown eyes. "I know."

She seemed in better spirits today than she had since before the accident. The color had returned to her cheeks and the circles under her eyes had disappeared. Faith had been tempted to wake her for dinner the night before, but she was glad she had let Annie sleep. She'd been ravenous at breakfast, though, devouring a stack of blueberry pancakes and several links of sausage.

Jackie met them at the door. "Thank God you left Bitsy at home." She stepped out of the way and waved them in.

Faith's stomach churned. Her sister's mood was worse than she'd anticipated. "Give me some credit, Jackie. I realize my child is better off at a friend's house than here with us, discussing a very sensitive grown-up issue."

Jackie ushered them into the dining room where Bill, Cooper, and Sam stood around the antique double-pedestal table.

Faith greeted Sam with an air kiss beside her cheek. "Where's Eli? Any news on his case?"

Eli had called Mike the previous evening and warned them to keep close tabs on Annie until Thea's brothers were in custody. "The Bell brothers are out for revenge. I don't want Annie getting caught in the cross fire."

"Understood," Mike had said. "But you don't need to worry about Annie. At least not tonight. She's sound asleep in bed. Has been since she got home from school."

Sam cast a quick glance at Annie to make sure she was out of earshot. "Not yet. I'll let you know as soon as I hear something. It's probably best if she doesn't hang out with Thea until this is over."

Faith and Sam watched Annie walk around the table to speak to Cooper. Annie said something to him, and he leaned down and whispered something in return.

"Watch out. The kettle is about to boil." Sam nodded at Jackie who was standing next to them, glaring at Annie.

When Annie covered her mouth to hide her smile, Jackie's face turned purple. "There is nothing funny about this situation."

"Geez, Mom. Lighten up," Cooper said.

"I'll lighten up when this unpleasant business is behind us."

Sam tossed her hands in the air. "I almost forgot. I have something for you, Annie." She removed a gift-wrapped package the size of a small book from her bag and walked it around the table. Sam said something to Annie that Faith couldn't hear.

"Thanks," Annie said, her face now serious as she slipped the gift inside her own bag.

"If you're finished with this little gift exchange, I'd like to get started." Jackie pulled out the chair in front of her. "Annie, you sit here with Mike and Faith, and I'll sit across from you with my husband and son." She circled the table to the other side.

"I guess that leaves me down here." Sam took a seat at the head of the table. "Does that mean I'm the mediator?"

Faith relaxed a little at the idea of Sam acting as referee.

"We probably need a mediator," Jackie said. "Just make sure your vote is impartial."

Cooper stared at her in disbelief. "What is wrong with you, Mom? This is not an election. We're not going to cast votes."

Bill rested a hand on his son's shoulder. "Why don't we all have a seat and talk about the situation in a calm manner?"

Everyone sat down in their appointed chairs.

"Before we begin," Sam said, eyeing their older sister, "I suggest we retract the claws and the fangs, and remember that we're a family. We love both of you very much." She looked first at Annie and then at Cooper. "The purpose of this meeting, as I understand it anyway, is to voice our feelings and come up with a solution that works for everyone."

Everyone nodded their agreement.

Sam rested her arms on the table and steepled her fingers. "Then let's start by looking at the big picture. We have two options—terminating the pregnancy or carrying the baby to term." She focused her attention on Annie. "When we spoke last weekend, you were thinking about terminating the pregnancy. Is this still a consideration?"

"Not anymore." Annie looked over at Cooper who nodded for her to continue. "I've had a chance to think about it, and that is not what I want for this baby."

"You don't get to make that decision alone," Jackie said.

"Actually, she does," Faith said. "It's her body. Mike and I are Annie's legal guardians. We agree it's in her best interest to see the pregnancy through, whether she raises the baby on her own or places it up for adoption."

"I'm sorry to disappoint you, Faith, but the three of us"— Jackie gestured at her husband and son—"are adamantly opposed to marriage. Cooper and Annie are still children themselves. Having this baby will ruin their lives."

"Then it sounds to me like adoption is the most viable solution," Faith said.

When Annie tapped Faith on the arm and whispered, "I'm going to the bathroom," Faith scooted her chair over to make room for Annie to get out.

"You can't wait to get your hands on this baby, can you, Faith? Well I have news for you. This is not about your desire for another child."

Cooper gritted his teeth. "I hate to say it, Mom, but adoption makes the most sense."

"What are you saying?" Jackie shifted to face her son. "We talked about this at length last night, and we agreed that an abortion is the best solution for everybody. We will pay for the procedure, get her the best medical care, and then the two of you can move on with your lives."

"I never agreed to that. You agreed to that for me." He looked down the table at Sam. "For the record, Aunt Sam, terminating the pregnancy is not what I want."

Faith's heart pounded against her ribcage. "I don't believe you, Jackie. You're saying you'd rather kill an innocent fetus than give some loving parents a chance at having a baby. I'm not talking about Mike and me specifically, although us adopting the baby makes the most sense."

"And have my grandchild raised by my sister?" Jackie cried. "I don't think so."

"Quiet!" Sam yelled, pounding her fist on the table. "Fighting about it is not making this any easier for Annie." Her eyes traveled to Annie's empty chair. "Where is she anyway?"

"She went to the bathroom," Faith said.

They glared across the table at one another while they waited for Annie to return. When five minutes passed and still no Annie, Faith got up to check on her.

She checked the bathrooms downstairs, but they were all empty. When she didn't find her in any of the family rooms, she ran upstairs and searched the bedroom floor. She returned to the table. "I can't find her anywhere. She must have left. I hope you're happy, Jackie. You ran the poor kid off to God knows where. She has broken ribs, a wounded shoulder, and she's pregnant. She's already scared to death. You only made it worse by ranting and raving like some kind of lunatic."

Cooper pushed back from the table and went to stand behind Sam. "This is all my fault for letting things get out of hand. I should have told you sooner. Annie and I have already made our decision. We went to Sandy's last night for ice cream and had a serious heart-to-heart talk about every possible option. We agreed that the best thing for this baby, *our* baby, is to find loving parents who can provide a good home."

"But—" Jackie started to protest.

He turned his back on his mother. "Honestly, Aunt Faith, I have mixed emotions about you and Mike raising my child. But that doesn't mean Annie and I aren't willing to consider the possibility. We have plenty of time for that later. For now, I need to find Annie." And with that, Cooper turned around and headed straight for the door.

## TWENTY-EIGHT

ANNIE

A nnie knew the minute she sat down at the table that things would not go her way at Jackie's so-called meeting. She removed her phone from her bag and texted Thea under the table: "*Help! Can you come pick me up?*" She typed out Jackie's address and added: "*I'll meet you at the end of the driveway.*"

She waited ten minutes, until the real bickering began, before sneaking out the front door. She removed her vial of painkillers from her bag and popped two, twice the recommended dosage, into her mouth. She swallowed them with saliva. She'd stopped taking the meds days ago, but she was desperate for the pain to stop. The throbbing in her shoulder and ribs had eased up days ago. But the pangs she experienced in her chest were unbearable. She was single-handedly tearing the Sweeney family apart, and that felt like a knife ripping her heart to pieces.

Annie hurried down the long driveway with tears flooding her eyes and streaming down her cheeks. She was relieved to see Thea's clunker parked on the side of the road. She winced at the pain in her shoulder as she climbed in the car.

"What's wrong?" Thea asked when she saw Annie's tears. She

dug in the center console for a travel package of tissues. "Did someone die?"

"Just drive!" Annie pointed at the road in front of them.

"You got it." Thea threw the car in gear and spun out toward town.

"This baby is ruining my life." Annie wrapped her arms around her belly and sobbed into a wad of tissues for the next several miles.

Finally, spent, she blinked away the tears. The road ahead of her stared back. Annie accessed the message app on her phone and clicked on the text she'd received from Heidi late Thursday afternoon: "*I met with Sam today on business. She shared your news with me. Don't be angry with her. She's concerned. I won't interfere unless you want me to. But know I'm here for you if you need anything at all.*"

She removed the brightly wrapped package from her bag.

"What's that?" Thea asked, eyeing the gift.

"I'm not sure. Heidi asked Sam to give it to me."

She tore open the attached note.

*My dearest Annie,*

*I am so terribly sorry about your accident. I take full responsibility for making you angry. If only I could relive those hours, that day, the past sixteen years. I will leave you alone for now, to give you the space you need to work through your feelings. My hope is we will one day reconcile our relationship, and forge the friendship we'd begun before all this happened.*

*The happiest time of my life was planning Sam's wedding with you back in December. Explore your talents. You have so many. My dream is for us to one day work together, a mother and daughter event planning team. I wanted you to have this photo album, a portfolio of my work. We can do great things together, if only you can find it in your heart to forgive me.*

*Heidi*

Annie ripped the paper off the small album, a miniature portfolio of Heidi's work in California, and thumbed through the index-sized photographs. The glitzy events Heidi had planned for her movie star clients didn't surprise her. She knew her mother had talent. Isn't that where she'd gotten hers?

She snapped the album shut. Annie had reached the end of her rope and had no one else to turn to. This baby had created a rift between the Sweeney sisters the size of the Grand Canyon. And it hadn't even been born yet. One wanted adoption. One insisted on abortion. Which left Sam to cast the deciding vote. Sam would take her side if Annie asked her to, but Annie refused to put her in the middle. She'd been wrong in thinking she could count on Cooper. Why hadn't he defended her against his mother? Jackie was mean and vicious and determined to get her way. But Annie didn't blame him. She was his mother.

"I see your parents haven't kicked you out of the house yet," she'd said to Cooper when she arrived at the meeting.

He'd smiled and said, "They're thinking of enlisting me in the Marines." His attempt at lightening the mood had made her laugh. Which, in turn, had infuriated Jackie.

His mother would stop at nothing to get her way, even if it meant cutting him off without a penny. Cooper was committed to doing the right thing, not because it was expected of him but because he was good and honest. He would sacrifice everything for her—his future, his inheritance, his family. But Annie couldn't let him do that.

"Which way?" Thea asked when she slowed to a stop at the light at the intersection of Creekside and Main.

"That way." Annie aimed her thumb at Main Street. "To the bus station."

Thea clicked on her left turn signal. "Where are you going once you get to the bus station, if you don't mind me asking?"

"To Charleston. To see Heidi."

Thea's amber eyes bulged. "Are you sure that's what you wanna do?"

Annie sat straight up in her seat. "I'm positive."

"In that case, I'll drive you," Thea said, placing both hands on the steering wheel as though preparing for a long road trip.

"I can't ask you to do that, Thea." She noticed her friend's uniform beneath her coat. "Don't you have to work, anyway?"

"I worked the morning shift. I was leaving The Grill when you texted."

"Are you sure?"

Thea nodded. "Positive."

Annie smiled. "In that case, I accept your offer."

---

They spent the forty-minute drive to Charleston strategizing on how best to handle her problem. Thea offered suggestions on alternative solutions, but without the support of the Sweeney family, none of them seemed feasible. Annie felt numb all over from the painkillers. She had enough pills to last her until Tuesday. Enough to get the job done and catch the next bus to New York City.

Ten minutes outside of Charleston, Annie sent Heidi a text: "*What is your address?*"

Heidi responded immediately with an address on Broad Street.

Annie plugged the address into her maps app, and Thea followed the voice navigation with ease. She pulled up against the curb across the street from the two story-house, the kind with the narrow side facing the street and the longer side stretching deep into the property.

Annie saw Heidi waiting for her on the second-floor side porch with a man, nice-looking with salt-and-pepper hair, standing next to her. Her lip curled up. "I wasn't expecting a boyfriend."

Heidi waved a cheerful greeting as though welcoming home her daughter from her first semester at college.

"You don't have to do this, you know." Thea said.

Annie gave an affirmative nod. "Yes, I do."

Thea put the car in neutral and killed the engine. "In that case, I'll wait for you here."

"If Heidi agrees to help me, I won't be going back to Prospect."

"Text me either way." Thea held up her cell phone. "I won't leave until I hear from you."

"You're a good friend, Thea. I hope one day I can repay the favor." Annie then maneuvered herself out of the sedan.

As Annie was crossing the street, Heidi cupped her hands around her mouth and called down to her, "Invite your friend to come up with you."

She kept walking. In a voice loud enough for Heidi to hear, she said, "Sorry to disappoint you. But this isn't a social call."

## TWENTY-NINE

# HEIDI

"Look at you, you poor thing." Heidi reached for Annie's good hand and felt her body quivering beneath her touch. "How're you feeling?"

Annie averted her gaze. "I've been better."

Heidi took ahold of Hugh's arm. "I'd like you to meet my friend Hugh Kelley. Hugh, this is Annie."

Annie relaxed a little and forced her lips into a thin smile. "It's nice to meet you, Mr. Kelley."

"Please. Call me Hugh," he said, offering a warm smile in return. "I've heard a lot of nice things about you. Well . . ." He shoved his hands into his pockets. "I should leave the two of you to talk. I'll be downstairs if you need me." He gave Heidi a parting kiss on the cheek.

Annie watched him disappear down the stairs. "Does he live here?"

"He owns the house. I rent this upstairs apartment from him. Why don't we go inside where it's warm?" Heidi held the door open for Annie, and the two went inside. Heidi then turned to her and said, "Can I take your coat?"

She gripped her fleece tighter around her body. "Thanks, but I'll leave it on for now. It's hard to get off with my shoulder."

Heidi realized then that Annie had her bad arm through the sleeve of her coat and the sling tied around her neck on the outside of the fleece.

"Would you like something to drink? Maybe some hot chocolate or a cup of tea."

Annie licked her dry lips. The painkillers gave her cotton mouth. "Some water would be nice. If you don't mind."

"Sure. I'll just be a minute." Heidi went to the adjoining kitchen, and while she filled a tall glass with water from her Brita pitcher, she watched her daughter out of the corner of her eye. Annie wandered around the room, stopping to peek out the window before moving on to scrutinize Heidi's framed photographs on the console table behind the sofa. She held her breath when her daughter picked up a photograph of a much younger Heidi holding a minutes-old infant—the only picture she owned of the two of them together.

Rounding the counter that separated the two rooms, she handed Annie the glass of water. "Come, let's sit down." She led her to the sofa and waited until they were both seated. "Since this isn't a social call, tell me why you're here."

Annie gulped down half the glass of water. "You said in your text, if I ever needed anything . . ." Her voice trailed off.

Heidi nodded. "And I meant it. How can I help?"

"I don't know where else to turn." Annie drained the rest of the water and set the glass down on the coffee table. "I can't have this baby, Heidi. I need someone to sign the forms so I can get an abortion. Since you're my biological mother, I was hoping you would consent."

Heidi's mind raced. This was not what she'd expected. "Why did you come to me? Why not ask Faith or Mike to help you? They're your legal guardians."

"They don't approve of me having an abortion. They want me to have the baby so they can adopt it."

"Oh. I see." Heidi did not think legal guardians adopting their charge's baby was ethical, but it was not her place to question the arrangement. At least not yet. *Play your cards right,* she reminded herself.

"No, you don't see," said Annie, her eyes dark with anger.

Heidi recognized the eyes that were so much like her father's, and the temper that smoldered just beneath the surface. "Then tell me."

"The whole Sweeney family is arguing over this baby. Jackie insists I have an abortion, but she doesn't have the authority to sign the consent form. I wanna make the whole thing go away, so everyone will stop fighting."

"What does Cooper want?"

"We talked about it for a long time last night. And we agreed that adoption was the best thing for our baby. But then today, at the meeting, he refused to speak up."

A chill traveled Heidi's spine. "Wait a minute. What meeting?"

"Jackie arranged a meeting this afternoon at her house to talk about the baby. They were all so busy yelling at each other, they didn't realize that excusing myself to go to the bathroom was really a ploy to escape all the quarreling."

Heidi puckered her hot-pink lips. "I see." It hardly seemed fair to put a sixteen-year-old girl in Annie's predicament on the spot like that. She wasn't completely surprised at Jackie's behavior. True, she hadn't seen Jackie since Sam's wedding reception, since the contents of her spilled purse had revealed her true identity. But before that, while Jackie had been pleasant to work with, on more than one occasion Heidi had sensed edginess behind the decorator's public persona.

Annie cast a nervous glance at the door. "Are you gonna help me or not? My ride is waiting."

Heidi hesitated. She couldn't make such an important decision without further consideration. "Can you give me a chance to think about it? I don't like to make such important decisions without at least sleeping on it first."

"Oh really?" Annie brought her body to its full height. "How many nights did you sleep on your decision to abandon me?"

Heidi jerked her head back as though she'd been slapped. "I guess I deserved that." She hesitated. She wanted Annie's forgiveness more than anything she'd ever wanted in her life. But she wouldn't go along with something she disapproved of to get it. "I'm sorry, Annie. If I have to decide now, the answer is no."

Annie's mouth dropped open. "But you said . . ."

"I understand you're upset." Heidi tucked a strand of Annie's hair behind her ear. "But give me a chance to explain. I was once a girl, not much older than you, in your same plight. Looking at you now, at the lovely young woman you've become—without any help from me, I might add—I can't, in good conscience, help you terminate your pregnancy. We are talking about a baby here, Annie, a living human being that will have your beautiful brown eyes and honey-colored hair. A child that will make her mark on the world, much like you're making yours with your delightful manner, creative flair, and willingness to help others."

Annie's lip quivered.

Heidi massaged Annie's good shoulder. "You've had a traumatic day, honey. You're in a fragile state of mind. Five minutes ago, you told me that you and Cooper had decided to put the baby up for adoption. You're letting Jackie pressure you into something you aren't prepared to do." Heidi inched closer. "Tell you what. Why don't you stay here with me tonight? We can have dinner together. We'll go out somewhere. Or better yet, we'll cook here. We can make pasta or concoct some sort of chowder. I have a couple of recipes I've been dying to try out. We'll both get a good night's sleep and talk more about this in the morning."

Annie rubbed the back of her neck. "I'm not sure I'm ready for that."

"I decorated my guest room with you in mind, hoping one day you'd consider coming to live with me. It's yours for as long as you need it. If you decide to have the baby, you can count on me both before and after the baby is born. I'll help you find the right adoption agency, or, if you want to keep the baby, I'll help you raise it. I would do just about anything to make it up to you, for walking out on you and your father. But I can't do this. You would end up hating me, honey. And you'd end up hating yourself."

## THIRTY

ANNIE

Annie took the porch steps two at a time on the way down and dashed across the street to Thea's car. She jumped in the car and slammed the door.

"Girl! Am I ever glad to see you. I didn't realize it but my phone is dead." Thea held up her phone to show Annie the black screen. "I was getting ready to come in there after you."

"Let's just get out of here!" Annie said, struggling to strap the seat belt over her injured arm.

"Yes, ma'am." Thea started the engine. "Where to?"

"Anywhere but here. Just get me away from her." Annie collapsed against the seat, squeezing her eyes tight.

They rode in silence until after they'd crossed the Ashley River bridge. "What happened?" Thea asked at last. "Did she refuse to help you?"

"Sorta. She offered to help me, just not the kinda help I need. 'Come live with me,'" she said, mocking Heidi in a squeaky voice. "'I'll help you raise the baby. I have a spare bedroom for you.'" Annie lowered her voice to normal. "She's just like everyone else. She's trying to use this baby to get what she wants."

Thea kept her eyes on the road. "Don't get mad at me for

saying this, but I'm glad she didn't agree to the abortion. I don't think that's what you really want."

Annie removed a tissue from the package Thea had given her earlier and blew her nose. "What I really want is for my life to go back to the way it was. And the only way I know to do that is to get an abortion."

"That's not gonna happen, Annie. The sooner you accept that your life has changed forever, the better off you'll be. Would it really be so bad to live with Heidi?"

"Honestly, I'd rather move back to Florida to the worst apartment my father and I ever stayed in." She let out a deep breath, allowing the tension to drain from her body. "But living with Heidi might be my only choice. At least she has a nice apartment."

"You're scared and confused and you need a place to hole up for a while. Things will look clearer after a few days. Why don't you come home with me?"

Thea was right. Annie needed time on neutral ground where she could think without everyone telling her what to do. What she really needed was Flora's calm voice of reason assuring her that everything would be okay. Faith would freak when she found out Annie was staying with Thea. She glanced down at the phone she held gripped in her hand. She thumbed through the missed calls and text messages from Cooper, Faith, and Sam, begging her to come home. There was even an apology from Jackie, although Annie questioned her sincerity. She rolled down the window and hurled the phone on the pavement into the lane of oncoming traffic.

Thea's golden eyes stared at her as if she'd lost her mind. "What'd you do that for? Are you crazy?"

"That's actually the sanest thing I've done in a while. Jackie bought me that phone when I first came to Prospect. I'd never owned a phone before, and I'd always gotten along just fine."

"You go, girl," Thea said, holding her hand up for a high five.

She slapped her friend's hand. "You know what I need right now? Comfort food," Annie said without waiting for Thea to respond. "And I'm buying."

"I'm down with that," Thea said, and pulled into the next McDonald's.

They each ordered a chocolate milkshake and split a large order of fries. "I've gotta stop eating like this," Annie said, her mouth stuffed with french fries. "I'm gonna be fat as a hog come summertime."

"You're eating for two. At least you have an excuse," Thea said, sucking on the straw of her shake.

"As if I could forget," she mumbled.

***

Annie slept the rest of the way home to Prospect. When they arrived at Thea's house, she was relieved to see the driveway empty. With any luck, she'd avoid another encounter with Thea's brothers. She had no intention of staying long. Just long enough to figure out a plan for her future. She had a meager savings in her bank account from working at Sweeney's, which was enough to buy her a bus ticket to New York but not much else.

"I hope your mom doesn't mind me staying here," Annie said as they climbed the front steps.

"Mama? Are you kidding me? She'll be thrilled."

Thea inserted her key in the lock and swung the front door open. Annie knew right away that something wasn't right. The lights were turned down low and the floor pulsed from the rap music blasting from MTV. Through the haze of cigarette smoke, Annie made out the shapes of two bodies, one kicked back in Flora's recliner and one slumped over in a chair against the wall near the TV.

"Close that door, damnit. It's cold out there." Tyrone leapt over the back of the sofa, and slammed the door shut, twisting the deadbolt into the lock position. He leaned back against the door. "We've been waiting for you."

Thea's brow scrunched up. "Why? What're y'all even doing here? And where's your car?"

"Ours is in the shop," Willie said from across the room. "We need to borrow yours."

She propped a fist on her hip. "Then how am I supposed to get around?"

"You'll figure out a way," Willie said.

Thea shifted her gaze back and forth between her brothers. "Where's Mama?"

"We sent *Mama* to her room." Tyrone let out a cackle of laughter that sent a chill down Annie's spine. "You might say she was misbehaving."

"Humph. Looks to me like the two of you are the ones misbehaving."

Annie followed Thea's gaze to the coffee table, which was littered with crumpled beer cans, a half-empty bottle of liquor, and an ashtray overflowing with cigarette butts. Annie had never done drugs before, but she knew enough to suspect the lines of white powder laid out on a framed photograph of MLK was cocaine.

"I better go check on Mama. She might need her insulin." Thea took a step forward, but Tyrone grabbed her arm and held her back. "Not so fast, little sister. You might not like what you see."

Thea's eyes bulged. "What'd you mean? What'd you do to her?"

"We didn't do nuttin to her," Willie said. "She was like that when we got here. All passed out in her bed like she were dead. Except I know she ain't dead cause of the sweat on her forehead."

Thea tugged at her arm but Tyrone tightened his grip, refusing to let her go. "What's wrong with you? Why didn't you call an ambulance?"

Willie shrugged. "We haven't gotten around to it yet."

Thea lifted her leg and brought the heel of her work shoe down on Tyrone's foot, startling him. She yanked her arm free and darted across the room toward a hallway that Annie suspected led to the bedrooms. Annie heard a popping sound and saw her friend drop to her knees, covering her head and ears with her hands and screaming, "Don't shoot me! Please dear god, don't shoot me." Chunks of plaster rained down on her from where the bullet had lodged in the ceiling above her head.

Annie stood paralyzed in place. She felt Tyrone's hand pressing against the small of her back, his breath tickling her neck, and his lips close to her ear. "We gonna have ourselves some fun *to-night*, Annie girl."

## THIRTY-ONE

## COOPER

Cooper had been driving around for two hours searching for Annie. He'd gone to all the places he thought she might be. Except to the one place he was certain he'd find her. He didn't know where Thea lived. He didn't even know who to ask for her address. Thea didn't have any friends other than Annie. At least as far as he knew. And Annie had only a few friends, all of them family aside from Thea. Some friend he'd turned out to be. He'd allowed his mother to come down hard on her, and he'd done nothing to stop her.

The driving had taken the edge off his anger. He'd been furious with his mother earlier. She'd followed him to his car when he walked out of the meeting, barking orders at him and forbidding him to leave the property.

He'd stopped dead in his tracks. "What did you say?" He slowly turned to face her.

Jackie stood tall, her spine ramrod straight, her jaw clinched. "I *said*, I forbid you to leave this property."

He stepped up close to her and looked directly into her eyes. "Sean and I paid for that Cruiser ourselves. I'll drive it any damn where I want to."

"Not while I'm paying for the insurance," she said, her head bobbing back and forth.

"Nice try, but Dad pays for the insurance." He leered down at her. "This is all your fault. If you hadn't pressured her like that."

"You're as much to blame as I am. We agreed to present a united front."

"I never agreed to anything. I made that perfectly clear last night. You got that all mixed up in your delusional mind." He rounded the Cruiser to the driver's side and opened the door. "I'm going to find Annie and you can't stop me." He got in the Cruiser and slammed the door without giving her a chance to respond.

His dad called him about an hour later, while he was searching for Annie. "I'm sorry, son. I let things get out of control. Your mom's . . . well, she's not thinking clearly right now."

"No shit, Dad. Can't you do something to calm her down?"

"I already did. I gave her a tranquilizer and sent her to her room for a nap. I'll talk to her when she gets up." His father paused and Cooper was tempted to end the call. "I was wrong to go along with her. All I could think about was how a baby would ruin your future. But you're right. We have to put the baby's health and well-being first. You reminded me how important it is to do the right thing."

He sounded sincere but Cooper wasn't ready to forgive him just yet. His father had betrayed him by going along with his mother. "You shouldn't need reminding. You're the one who taught me that."

"Grown-ups sometimes lose their way too. Thanks for straightening me out. I'm proud of you, Coop. You're turning into a fine young man. I have no doubt you are trying to do what's right. I have no doubt you are trying to make the best decision you can. I'm with you on this, regardless of your mother's position."

"You just take care of Mom, and let me worry about Annie."

The last thing Cooper wanted was to come between his parents. Nearly two years had passed since their close encounter with divorce. His parents had tried to hide Bill's affair, but Cooper and Sean knew all about Daisy Calhoun. They'd been counselors at a camp in the North Carolina mountains that summer, but when they'd gotten home, their friends had told them all about the woman with the fake yellow hair and big breasts they'd seen driving around town in their father's convertible. Jackie's midlife crisis was partially to blame for the breakup of their marriage. For years she'd exhibited behavior much like what Cooper had seen from her in the past two days. It wasn't until she'd gone off to Charleston and started her own design firm that she became a new and improved woman. She'd forgiven his father and they had been acting like newlyweds ever since.

Cooper tossed his cell phone onto the passenger seat. "Don't worry, Dad," he said out loud in the empty car. "I'll figure this thing out on my own."

He made a sudden U-turn and headed in the opposite direction. A quarter mile down the road, he made a left-hand turn onto a gravel driveway. Cooper felt a huge sense of calm as soon as he crossed the threshold into Sam's bungalow. His mother liked to cram every surface in their house with knickknacks, but Sam's home was uncluttered. Her contemporary furniture, upholstered in soft grays and blues, set him at ease. Who wouldn't want to live in a place like this, where every room offered a view of the inlet he loved so much. He wouldn't find anything like this in New York City.

"Come here, you." The last of his tension drained from his body when Aunt Sam embraced him. He was mentally and physically exhausted, but he'd come to the right place. She held him at arm's length. "Any luck in finding Annie?"

"Not yet. I was hoping you'd heard from her."

Faith left the sofa where she'd been sitting and came to greet him. "We've texted and called. She's avoiding us."

"Maybe we should check Annie's Find My iPhone app," Cooper suggested.

"We already did that," Faith explained. "The phone isn't showing up. I guess that means the battery is dead or the phone is turned off."

"Thea gave me her cell number when Annie was in the hospital after the accident," Sam said. "We've been texting and calling her as well with no luck."

"Thea is the reason I'm here," Cooper said. "I'm hoping Eli can help me figure out where she lives."

"He's out conducting a search of his own. He should be back any minute. Come over here and sit down." Sam looped her arm through his and walked him over to the sitting area in front of the fireplace. "Can I offer you something to drink, maybe a cup of tea?"

"No, but thanks." When he lowered himself to the sofa, his aunts sat down on either side of him. "I'm sure Annie is fine. She's probably hanging out at Thea's house, waiting for everyone to calm down before she comes home."

Cooper noticed the uncertain glance Faith cast her sister. "What are you not telling me?"

"Well . . ." Sam crossed her legs. "Eli's been working a big case that involves Thea's brothers. He busted up their prostitution ring yesterday. Thea's brothers got away. Eli's men confiscated a large supply of drugs from the property and brought in a number of men and women for questioning. Unfortunately, no one could provide any leads on the Bell brothers."

"The police have an APB out on them now," Faith said. "As you can imagine, they aren't too happy with the police at the moment. They're aware of Eli's relationship with Annie. Which makes us worry they'll come after her in retaliation."

"What a nightmare." Cooper sank back against the sofa. "I

assume Eli knows where Thea lives. Has he checked to see if Annie's there?"

Sam nodded. "He knows where Thea lives and I'm sure he's been by there, but I don't know what he found out." They heard the sound of gravel crunching in the driveway. "That's probably him now."

The somber expression on Eli's face when he came through the front door drove Cooper off the couch. "Did you find Annie? Was she at Thea's house? Have her brothers threatened Annie?"

Eli gripped Cooper by the arms. "Take a deep breath and calm down. So far, I have no news. Let's sit down and I'll tell you what I know." He spun Cooper around and walked him back to the sofa. "Yes, I have been twice to Thea's house today." Eli took a seat in the chair beside him. "There are not any cars in the driveway, and no one is answering the door. Which concerns me because Thea's mother suffers from diabetes. I'd go so far as to call her a shut-in."

Sam's cell phone vibrated on the coffee table in front of them. Four sets of eyes locked in on the caller ID. Sam smacked her forehead. "Why didn't we think to call Heidi?" She snatched up the phone. "Have you seen Annie?" Sam's blue eyes narrowed as she listened to what Heidi was saying. "Oh, thank God. Hang on. I'm going to put you on speakerphone. I'm here with Faith, Eli, and Cooper." Sam held the phone away from her mouth. "Annie left Heidi's house twenty minutes ago." She clicked her speaker icon and set the phone back down on the coffee table. "You're on speaker now, Heidi. Did you happen to see who Annie was with?"

"Not exactly. She was with another girl who was driving an Oldsmobile in worse shape than my Mustang."

"That's Thea," Sam said. "That's what we suspected."

"Annie wanted me to sign the forms so she can have an abortion," Heidi said. "She stormed out of here when I wouldn't give her my consent. I got the impression that's not what she really wants."

"I agree," Sam said. "She's too upset to know what she really wants right now."

"What were y'all thinking putting the poor girl on the spot like that?" Heidi asked. "No wonder she took off."

Cooper moved to the edge of the sofa, closer to the phone. "Heidi, it's Cooper. I'm responsible for this whole mess. My mother isn't thinking straight right now. I should have stopped the meeting from taking place."

Heidi let out an audible sigh. "Don't blame yourself, honey. The grown-ups in this situation need to put their feelings aside and focus on what's best for you, Annie, and the baby."

"Point taken, Heidi. And agreed. It's Faith by the way. Do you know where Annie and Thea may have gone?"

"I assume they were headed back to Prospect. But she didn't say. For the record, I offered for Annie to live here with me. For a few days or until after the baby comes. I even told her I'd help raise it if that's what she decides to do."

Faith's eyes were glassy with tears. "Thank you, Heidi. That might be her best option, considering all the stress around here."

"Should I come down there and help you look for her?" Heidi asked in an anxious tone.

Eli said, "I think it's better if you stay there, at least for now, in case she returns."

"That makes sense," Heidi said. "But I'll be worried out of my mind. Will you stay in touch, please, Sam? Let me know the minute you find her?"

"Of course. And you do the same if you hear from her first." Sam punched the button and ended the call. "So now we know where Annie is."

Eli consulted his watch. "According to Heidi, they left Charleston around five-thirty. I'll give them a few minutes before heading back over to Thea's house."

Cooper perked up. "Can I go with you?"

"Not this time, bud. Things might get a little dicey. I need you to stay here and take care of the women." Eli winked at Sam, and she flashed him a stubborn I-don't-need-anyone-to-take-care-of-me look in return.

## THIRTY-TWO

## ELI

Thea's Cutlass was parked in the driveway when Eli arrived at the Bell home. He retraced his steps from earlier and rapped his knuckles on the front door. When no one answered, he pounded harder.

"Thea," he called out. "It's Eli Marshall. Is Annie with you? I need to speak to her for a minute. Her family is worried about her."

A muffled voice answered from inside. "Go away, pig. We don't want none."

Eli cupped his hands around his mouth and spoke to the door. "I don't want any trouble, Tyrone. Or Willie. Whichever one of you is in there. Send Annie out and we'll be on our way."

"This is Tyrone, but Willie's in here too. If you leave peacefully, we won't have to hurt you. Annie don't wanna go with you. She's staying here with me. We gonna have ourselves a party."

Eli's mind raced. He considered breaking down the door, but realized that was dangerous without having any backup. "I'll consider going along with that if that's really what Annie wants. But I need for her to come out and tell me so herself."

Two shots rang out from within the house, followed by piercing screams. Eli dove off the stoop and into the bushes, scrambling for cover. He removed his radio from his waistband and signaled to dispatch for backup. "Shots fired. I repeat, shots fired." He barked out the address, and then crawled his way through the tunnel of overgrown shrubs around the side of the house. Crouching down, he ran across the yard to the adjacent wooded lot. Heart racing and lungs gasping for air, he hid behind a large pine tree. He heard the steady thump of rap music coming from inside the house three hundred feet away.

"Goddamnit!" He punched the tree and then winced in pain. He'd understood the risks involved. He was an officer of the law. But his obsession with sending the Bell brothers to prison had made him careless. And now, because of him, Annie's life was in danger.

He darted from one tree to the next as he made his way out of the woods. A line of five patrol cars sped down the road several minutes later and skidded to a halt in front of him. He rounded the rear end of the front car and slid into the passenger side next to Brad.

"Are you all right, man? "Brad's eyes traveled Eli's body. "You're not hurt anywhere, are you?"

"I'm fine. But Annie's inside the house with Tyrone and Willie Bell. When I asked them to let her come out, they fired shots." Eli quickly briefed Brad on Annie's friendship with Thea Bell. "To complicate matters, Annie is recovering from shoulder surgery as a result of her accident last week. And she's pregnant."

"Man, that sucks." Brad ran his hand over the top of his nearly bald head. "Do we have any idea who else is in the house?"

"I assume Flora, their mother, is in there with them."

"Their mother?" Brad repeated, his mouth agape. "Why would she let her sons get away with this?"

"I don't know," Eli said. "The Flora I once knew operated a

strict ship. But her diabetes has made her an invalid. Which worries me for her safety." Eli pointed at the road in front of them. "Drive up a little. I'm going to talk to them through the bullhorn, see if I can get them to cooperate."

Brad inched the patrol car forward. Eli got out and, hunkering down, shot off across the yard to the end of the dirt driveway where he'd left his squad car. He popped the trunk and removed a bulletproof vest, a pair of binoculars, and a megaphone. He slipped on the vest and crept up the side of his car, squatting down when he reached the front end. He lifted the bullhorn to his mouth. "Tyrone! Willie! It's Eli again. Let's see if we can work this thing out. Can you come out so we can talk?"

The volume on the music died and the front door swung open. Tyrone appeared in the doorway, using Annie's body as a shield. He held his right arm wrapped around her neck while his left hand pointed a pistol to her temple.

Eli lifted the binoculars and focused them on Annie. Her eyes were shut tight and her face scrunched up in fear.

"I ain't got nuttin to say to you, man." Tyrone's wild eyes darted around the yard. "You fucked with me, now you gonna pay." He kissed the side of Annie's head, near her ear. "Or maybe I'll make this little beauty suffer for you."

"This is between you and me, Tyrone. No reason to hurt her. Can't you see she's already been hurt enough?"

Tyrone tightened his grip on Annie. "If she behaves herself, I won't have to clip her other wing."

"Is Flora in there with you, Tyrone? Does she need medical attention?"

"My mama's health ain't none of your business. I'm warning you!" He fired a shot at the sky. "Get on outta here if you ever want to see this pretty little angel alive again." He yanked Annie back inside and slammed the door.

Eli climbed into the passenger side and shimmied over the console to the driver's seat. He started the engine and backed the car out of the driveway and down the street a hundred feet in the opposite direction from the other patrol cars. He radioed Swanson. "We need to isolate the area. You seal off your side of the road and I'll tape mine. Don't let anyone through for any reason, except the rescue squad and fire department. I'm calling in the hostage negotiators."

## THIRTY-THREE

ANNIE

Annie sat in the corner with her knees against her chest and her face tucked in the crook of her good arm. She could still feel the metal barrel of the gun Tyrone had pressed against her temple. She couldn't stop her teeth from chattering. But she wasn't cold. The tiny sitting room was stifling. The cigarette smoke made her want to gag and her armpits were damp with sweat. She needed Thea's help to get her injured arm out of the fleece, but she was too terrified to ask. She didn't want to draw attention to herself. Willie and Thea occupied opposite ends of the sofa, and Tyrone was stretched out in Flora's recliner, pointing the remote at the TV as though he was watching the Super Bowl instead of holding three innocent people hostage.

"I need me some food." Tyrone smacked his lips. "Thea, make yourself useful and rustle me up some grub. Make me some eggs over easy, bacon, and biscuits with honey." He waved his pistol in Annie's direction. "And take her with you. All that teeth chattering is grating my nerves."

Annie slowly rose to her feet and followed Thea into the kitchen. She heard Tyrone tell his brother, "Go in there with them, you idiot, in case they try something stupid."

Willie shuffled into the kitchen and plopped down in a metal chair at the tiny table beside the back door. He slipped on his Beats headphones and thumbed through a playlist on his phone.

Thea removed the ingredients she needed for the meal from the refrigerator and lined them up on the counter. Annie leaned in close to Thea. "Are they going to kill us?" she whispered.

"I ain't gonna lie to you, girl. They're mean enough to shoot us both dead. I'm so sorry, Annie, for getting you into this mess."

"What are you talking about? You didn't get *me* into anything. Tyrone has some kinda vendetta against Eli and he's taking it out on me. You're the one caught in the middle."

"I'm worried about my mama." She opened the drawer to the right of the stove and rummaged through the syringes. "Her insulin is gone. It was in here this morning. I don't care what they say. I'm gonna check on her." She turned off the stove and marched across the room. But Willie was too quick. He leapt out of his chair and blocked the door. "Where do you think you're going?"

Thea tried to push past him, but he wrapped his strong arms around her so she couldn't move.

"What's going on in there?" Tyrone hollered from the other room.

"Thea dropped an egg," Willie yelled back. "Nuttin for you to worry about. I'm just helping her clean it up."

"Tell her to hurry the fuck up. I'm hungry."

Willie dragged Thea away from the doorway. In a whisper loud enough for Annie to hear, he said, "I'm going to let you go so you can fix his food. If you make one wrong move, I'm gonna shoot you myself. Understood?"

Thea nodded, and he loosened his grip. She spun on her heels and elbowed him hard in the gut. "If anything happens to my mama, I'll be the one doing the shooting," she said to his bent-over body. "Do *you* understand?"

"Why you little cunt!" He tried to grab hold of her arm, but she wrenched herself free.

Thea returned to the stove, and Willie slumped back down in the chair, his head resting on his hand. She slammed cabinets and banged pots around as she prepared to cook.

"Keep it down in there, will ya?" Tyrone called, and the volume on the TV in the front room grew louder.

Annie handed her the ingredients as she needed them. Thea chunked a slab of butter in a cast iron skillet, and whisked the eggs in a bowl with milk. She poured the eggs into the skillet.

"What's wrong with your dumbass?" Thea spun around, turning her back on the eggs. Pointing her plastic spatula at Willie, she said, "I expect this kinda shit from him,"—she jerked her head toward the other room—"but not from you. If something happens to Mama or to Annie or me, you're gonna have our blood on your hands. Which means you're the one going to jail for life. Because he's gonna get off like he always does and let you take the fall."

Willie snorted. "Shut up, girl. You don't know what you're talking about. Tyrone's gonna find us a way out of here. We'll be long gone before morning."

"Ha. I wouldn't count on it," she said, scooping eggs out of the pan. She set a plate in front of Willie. "There's three of us in here and one of him out there. If we make a plan, we can get the gun away from him. Annie and I will tell the police that you helped us. Then you'll walk and he'll go to jail."

"Nice try, little sister, but it ain't gonna work. I'm already wanted on charges bigger than the ones I'm facing in here. Running is the only chance we got. If anybody dies in the process, then so be it." He waved her away. "Now get on out of here and take him his food."

Annie returned to her corner in the front room and balled herself up as tight as she could manage with her injured arm. The lingering smell of bacon caused her stomach to rumble. She should've asked for something to eat while she had a chance.

Tyrone scarfed down his food. Mopping up the last of his egg yolk with his remaining biscuit, he pushed his plate aside and leaned over the framed photograph of MLK on the coffee table, snorting up a line of white powder. "Time to party." He held the rolled-up dollar bill out to Annie. "Want some?"

"I don't do drugs," she said, and buried her face in her arm. *I'm freaking pregnant,* she wanted to scream. She wouldn't do drugs under normal circumstances. No way would she risk the health of her unborn baby. But hadn't she risked it anyway by coming here? Faith and Mike had tried to warn her. If only she'd listened.

"Come on, angel. You might as well have fun. I aim to have my way with you whether you like it or not."

"Leave her alone!" Thea picked up a throw pillow and hurled it at her brother. The pillow knocked the photograph off the coffee table and the cocaine spilled onto the brown shag carpet.

Tyrone shot out of his chair, bounded across the coffee table, and landed with the full weight of his body on his sister. He started throwing punches and Annie screamed. Willie rushed in from the kitchen. "Get off her, man!" he hollered, grabbing his brother by the shirt and hauling him off their sister. But it was too late. Tyrone had already busted her nose.

"Goddamnit, Thea! Look what you made me do." Tyrone went to the kitchen and returned with a rag and a bag of frozen peas. "This ain't like when we were little. We ain't playing games here. Willie and I are in big trouble. We need to figure a way out of this mess. And you need to stay out of our way while we doing it."

Holding the rag to her nose, Thea said, "Then why aren't you talking to them?" She aimed a thumb at the front of the house.

"You should be negotiating with the police instead of snorting that crap up your nose."

"We ain't ready to negotiate yet. They gonna sit out there and stew for a while, get good and worried about what's going on in here, before we tell them what we want."

"What do you want?" Annie asked in a meek voice.

Tyrone walked over to Annie and knelt down in front of her. He lifted her chin. "I want Eli to pay for ruining me. I had a good business going out at the farmhouse. All those fancy doctors and lawyers paying me the big bucks to get high and get them some pussy. I'm screwed, and it's all his fault."

Annie forced herself to meet his cold, hard eyes. "Whatever Eli did to you, he did because of his job. Please don't hurt him. He's a good police officer. He'll help you leave town if you let him."

"The only place he's gonna help me is into a maximum security prison. Come here, angel." He took Annie by the arm and helped her to her feet. He led her over to the sofa and pushed her gently down next to Thea. "Leave this nasty b'ness to me. If the two of you sit here together like good little girls, I won't have to hurt you."

"Can I go see Mama?" Thea asked.

"Nah, Thea. How many times I gotta tell ya? You can't go back there. Ain't nuttin for you to see, anyway. Mama's sleeping right now. We don't want to wake her up."

## THIRTY-FOUR

# ELI

The FBI hostage negotiator and his team arrived from Charleston in their mobile command center fifty minutes later. Logan Pomeroy's authoritative manner and intense green eyes studying him from behind thick lenses immediately set Eli at ease.

"I spoke with Chief Andrews on my way down," Pomeroy explained. "He has the utmost faith in your ability. Together, we will bring this situation to a close."

Eli nodded. The chief had flown to New Orleans that morning for his niece's wedding. He wasn't expected back until late the following evening. "You're in charge, sir. Just tell me what to do."

"Why don't we step into my office and I'll introduce you to my team." Pomeroy led Eli inside and introduced him to his second and third in command, whose names Eli didn't catch, stationed at a bank of controls that occupied one whole wall of the mobile unit.

"This is some setup you have," Eli said, impressed by the high tech systems in place.

"We're proud of it." Pomeroy gestured to a small worktable

and two chairs. "Why don't we sit down and you can tell us what you know."

Eli waited until Pomeroy was settled across from him. "As best we can tell, there are two suspects and three hostages inside the home." He told Pomeroy and his team about the Bell brothers' criminal history—including their alleged involvement in the prostitution and drug ring and the previous day's bust—and he explained his relationship with Annie and her friendship with the suspect's sister. "Although it has yet to be confirmed, we have reason to believe that Flora Bell, the suspects' mother, is also inside the house. She's in poor health. Diabetes."

"That complicates the situation for sure." Pomeroy took off his glasses and set them on the table. "All right, then. Let's start by interrupting their cell service. Get the local carriers on the line. Suspend service for everyone inside that house who owns a cell phone."

"We're on it, Chief," Second in Command said, swiveling around in his chair to face the computers.

Pomeroy rubbed his eyes and slipped his glasses back on. "While we're waiting, I'd like to get acquainted with the property." He produced a laptop and slid it across the table to Eli. Together they studied the Bells' lot and surrounding areas through both the county's website and Google Earth.

"Sir." Command Three spun around in his chair. "We've identified the carrier and suspended all cell service. Our men are in position. Are we prepared to proceed?"

"Affirmative."

Pomeroy and Eli left the table and went to stand behind Two and Three at command central. Two handed them headsets and they slipped them on. "I'll let you do the introductions," Pomeroy said. "We'll use the loudspeaker to make one last stab at getting our suspects to come out voluntarily."

Three nodded at Eli. "You're good to go."

All eyes focused on a large computer monitor that displayed a black-and-white image of the front of the house.

"Tyrone, Willie, it's Eli again. I hope you can hear me in there. I have someone here that would like to talk to you."

Pomeroy paused for a few seconds before he said, "Good evening, gentlemen."

Eli cringed at his choice of salutations. Then reminded himself that Pomeroy was the professional. He was merely trying to make nice.

"I'm Agent Logan Pomeroy with the FBI. Let's see if we can work this situation out so that everybody wins. But I need to know what it is you want so I can make that happen. Hold tight. We're bringing you a phone that will allow us to communicate."

On the monitor, they watched a cluster of armed and shielded agents creep up to the house, toss the phone through the window, shattering it, and back quickly away. Command Three made the connection and Eli heard the line ringing through his headset.

"The phone won't stop ringing until someone answers it," Pomeroy explained. "It takes awhile sometimes, but it eventually drives them nuts."

Five or six minutes passed before one of the Bell brothers accepted the call. "Let me speak to Eli."

Eli mouthed, "Tyrone," to Pomeroy.

"Tyrone, this is Agent Pomeroy, but I want you to call me Logan. Eli's standing right next to me. He's on the line with us."

"I'm here, Tyrone," Eli said.

"What'd you bring in the feds for?" Tyrone said in a gruff voice. "And what happened to my cell service?"

"We suspended the service," Pomeroy said. "You can have it back if you're willing to cooperate."

Tyrone let out a snort, then said, "Cooperate how?"

"By telling me what it is you want."

"Well . . . let's see. You can start by bringing me some Jack and coke. Throw in some cigs too. I'm down to my last one."

Pomeroy lifted his hand to his headset. "Come now, Tyrone. Work with me here. You know we can't bring you any booze or drugs. Are you okay on food? Do you need any medical supplies?"

"Nah, man. We done had supper. Go on home to your old lady and leave us alone."

"Can I speak to Willie?" Pomeroy asked.

"Willie's busy."

Pomeroy paused. "Does anyone need any medical attention in there?"

"Nope. Everybody's just dandy."

"How about your mother? She feeling okay? I understand she has a medical condition."

"Last time I checked, she was sleeping. I tried to wake her up, but she was conked out. She must be real tired."

Pomeroy's green eyes sought out Eli's. "Will you let my rescue crew come in for her? Just one stretcher and two men. I promise nobody else."

"No can do, G-man. My mama's just fine. She still breathing at least. The party is just getting started in here, and I ain't ready to negotiate yet. But I'll be sure to call you when I am. Not." They heard a cackle of laughter followed by the click of the call being disconnected.

The foursome watched the monitor in dismay as a black object, which could only be the phone, was tossed back through the broken window.

Pomeroy snatched off his headset. "Have our men surround the house. We're dealing with a psychopath. If he's willing to let his mother die, everyone else in there is in grave danger."

## THIRTY-FIVE

## FAITH

Mike was the first to arrive, bearing a deli tray from Harris Teeter and two loaves of bread—one wheat, one white. Faith relieved him of the tray. She had no sooner kicked the door shut behind him when the doorbell rang again. "I'll get it," Sam said, seeing that Faith's hands were full.

Heidi held out a wicker picnic basket, what Sam referred to as her tasty box. "I had some leftovers from an event I catered last night. I hope it's okay that I'm here."

Sam took the basket from her. "We wouldn't have asked you to come if we didn't want you here."

"Are you sure?" Her eyes were on Faith, who was still standing beside Sam.

Faith nodded. "Of course. Your place is here with us."

They heard the crunch of gravel and Bill's Mercedes with the vanity plates DRHART came into view. "Looks like we'll be feeding a crowd," Sam said. "Good thing you all brought food."

Bill and Sean greeted Sam and Faith with hugs. "Jackie's not feeling well," Bill said.

"I guess not, after her performance this afternoon," Sam mumbled.

Faith nudged her sister with her elbow. "We're just glad the two of you are here. Come on in. Cooper is in the kitchen."

They broke into small groups and migrated to the kitchen.

Considering the outcome of the afternoon's meeting, Faith thought it just as well Jackie stayed at home. But when she saw the disappointment that crossed Cooper's face, she understood just how hard the situation had been on him. He needed his mother's love and support now more than ever. Faith said a silent prayer—one of many offered to the Lord during the past few hours—that Jackie would realize the terrible mistake she was making before she ruined her relationship with her son.

Faith set the deli tray on the counter and removed the plastic lid. Then she retrieved condiments from the refrigerator and located paper plates, napkins, and forks from the pantry while Sam helped Heidi unpack her tasty box.

Sam clapped her hands and spoke to the crowd gathered in her kitchen. "Last we heard from Eli, they were waiting for the hostage team to arrive from Charleston. "Since there's not much else to do, we might as well eat. Thanks to Mike and Heidi we have plenty of food here." She gestured at the buffet spread out on the kitchen island.

They all loaded up a plate, but no one had much of an appetite. Mostly, they just picked at their food. Cooper and Sean sat at the table with Bill and Mike, the men's corner, while the women perched themselves on bar stools at the kitchen counter. Frequent glances at the clock on the stove and the watches on their wrists didn't make the time pass any quicker. They took turns pacing the floor, the movement offering a moment's relief from their restlessness. Sam brought out decks of cards and her favorite board games—Monopoly and Scrabble—but no one could concentrate enough to play.

When the doorbell rang around eight o'clock, Sam and Faith raced each other to answer it. Jackie stood in the doorway with a box of coffee in each hand and a stack of disposable cups tucked under her arm. "I thought you could use some caffeine. I understand if I'm not welcome here."

Sam took one of the boxes of coffee from Jackie. "You are always welcome in my home. You know that."

"I know one young man who will be thrilled to see you," Faith added.

Jackie's face lit up. "Do you think so, really? I'm not so sure."

Faith smiled. "Well, I have no doubt."

She looped an arm through each of her sister's and the threesome entered the kitchen together. Jackie's presence rendered the crowd momentarily silent.

"Caffeine, just what I need," Mike said when he spotted the coffee in her hand. "Jackie, you're my hero. Here, let me assist you with that." He stood and walked over to help her set up the coffee station on the counter beside the stove.

Once everyone had a steaming cup in hand, Jackie whistled for everyone's attention. "I know what you're all thinking, and I'm here to tell you that you're right. This nightmare is my fault. I don't know how to express my remorse for my behavior over the past few days. Saying I'm sorry seems inadequate. The one I owe the biggest apology to isn't here. Annie is a precious girl and I love her like my own child. I make no excuses except to say that I let my concern for my son's future cloud my judgment.

"It's hard to relinquish control of our children's lives. I guess we're all just beginning to learn that. But Cooper proved to me today that he is the compassionate and honorable young man we've raised him to be." She searched the crowd for her son's face. "I'm proud of you, son. Whatever you and Annie decide about the baby, I'm behind you a hundred percent." Her hazel eyes glassed over with unshed tears. "I only hope this situation comes to a rapid conclusion, so I can tell Annie myself how much she means to me. And to this family."

Faith went to stand beside her sister. "You're not the only one at fault here. You were right about me, Jackie. I couldn't wait to get my hands on that baby. I let my own desire to have another child get in the way of helping Annie make the decision that was right for her."

Mike coughed to clear his throat. "We are also to blame for not taking the threat from the Bell brothers seriously enough."

Sam stepped forward. "If anyone is responsible for putting Annie in danger, it's Eli. But I don't blame him. He risks his life every day to make the streets of Prospect a better place so friends like Annie and Thea can be safe when they visit each other's home."

"Amen to that," Faith said.

Sam continued. "Families disagree. It happens all the time. Lord knows we've had our share of arguments. But I know families who fuss and fight and hold grudges, folks who haven't spoken to their own siblings in decades. Not us. We're Sweeneys. Because we love each other, we forgive one another. We kiss and make up and move on. The important thing is, we're all here tonight, together, presenting a united front for Annie."

"And for Eli," Cooper added.

Sam nodded. "And for Eli."

"If I may . . ." Heidi raised her hand, her hot-pink fingernail pointing at the sky. "I'd just like to say . . . I'm certainly in no position to talk about parenting or family relationships. But I, too, have been selfish when it comes to Annie. Without regard for her feelings, I showed up out of the blue and demanded to be a part of her life,"—she tossed her hands out in front of her —"this life she'd worked so hard to create on her own. Annie has plenty of reasons to never see me again. And if that's what she wants, I will honor her wishes. But only because I know she's in good hands with you. It's clear to me how much you all love Annie. You've done so much for her—taken her into your homes, treated her like she's part of your family. And for that, I will always be grateful."

## THIRTY-SIX

ANNIE

Annie slept sitting straight up on the sofa. Rather, she pretended to sleep, hoping Tyrone would forget she was there. She took frequent peeks at him, monitoring his movements as he chain-smoked cigarettes, drank Jack Daniels straight from the bottle, and snorted his way through a mound of cocaine. She had no idea where this reserve stash had come from since Thea had dumped his previous supply on the floor.

Thea lay stretched out with her head in Annie's lap, her face now swollen and bruised. Willie had stopped partying hours ago. He sat in an upright chair in the corner watching a basketball game on TV. The roar of the crowd cheering, the squeak of rubber shoes against the court, and the excited voices of the anchormen commenting on each play could be heard throughout the house. The Tar Heels were beating the Wolfpack by six points with less than five minutes to go in the game. Whoever the Tar Heels and the Wolfpack were.

Annie had come to terms with her predicament. She understood the stakes. She'd mentally prepared herself, as best she could, to do whatever it took to survive, to protect the life of her unborn baby. Even if that meant letting Tyrone have his way with her. She saw how he'd treated Thea, his own sister. Annie couldn't bring herself to think about what he'd done to their mother.

It wouldn't be long now. He'd stubbed out his last cigarette, drained the last drops of whiskey, and snorted his last line of cocaine. Soon he would be looking for a different form of pleasure. She sensed his restlessness. He was all hyped up from the coke. Flicking his Bic lighter. Tapping his shoe on the floor. Reclining the chair, then bringing it upright, over and over again. When the time came, she would close her eyes and clear her mind of all thoughts except those of Cooper and their baby. She'd never wanted an abortion. What a pity she had to put the baby's life in danger for her to realize that.

At least two hours had passed since the hostage negotiator had tried to communicate with Tyrone. Annie had faith in Eli. She knew she could count on him to see the crisis through to the end. She imagined him pacing up and down the street out front, running his fingers through his dark curls, unable to get to Annie despite his close proximity to the house.

The buzzer on the TV sounded. The game had ended. The Tar Heels had won by two points.

"Keep an eye on Thea, will ya?" Tyrone said to Willie. "I'm gonna take angel girl to the back bedroom, and we gonna do our thing."

The recliner creaked and feet hit the floor. Tyrone tapped her lightly on the cheek. "Come on, Sleeping Beauty. Time to wake up now."

Annie opened her eyes and quickly shut them again at the sight of his menacing grin. *The baby, Annie. You must protect the baby at all cost.* She took a deep breath, but when she tried to get up, the sudden movement startled Thea from her sleep.

Thea bolted upright. When she saw her brother standing over them and realized what was happening, she flung herself backward into Annie's lap. "She's not going anywhere with you!" Thea said, her arms stretched wide in defense of her friend.

"Thea! Get the hell out of my way!" Tyrone cocked his arm back and smacked his sister on the side of her face.

Thea drew her knee in and kicked her brother square in the chest, sending him crashing against the wall behind him. "Run, Annie, run!" Thea jumped to her feet and made a dash for the bedroom hallway.

Annie scrambled over the back of the sofa. She was darting toward the door when she saw a flash of light and heard the crack of gunfire. The impact of the bullet propelled her forward, forcing her to the ground. The front door flung open, and men with machine guns, dressed in dark clothing with helmets on their heads and bulletproof vests covering their torsos, stormed the house. "Drop your weapons and get your hands in the air."

More shots rang out as bullets whizzed by her head. Somewhere on the floor close by, Thea screamed hysterically. The shooting stopped and Thea's cries for help diminished to a whimper.

"We need medical attention in here. Now!" a voice called.

Lying paralyzed and facedown on the floor, Annie saw legs in boot-clad feet hurrying past her. Finally, a pair of boots stopped in front of her. These were different than the others, still black but ankle height where the others were midcalf. She recognized these boots. And the lazy drawl of the person they belonged to. "Hang in there, honey." She felt a hand on her head, stroking her hair. "Help is on the way."

"Eli." Her mouth formed the word but no sound escaped her lips. *We've gotta stop meeting like this.* She closed her eyes and everything went black.

# THIRTY-SEVEN

## COOPER

Cooper's parents half-carried, half-dragged him out of the house to his father's sedan—his mother gripping his elbow and his father's arm circling his waist. They situated him in the bucket seat and buckled him up as though placing a toddler in a car seat. Sean crawled in beside him, placing a reassuring hand on his brother's forearm. Cooper couldn't remember the last time his family had ridden in the same car together. They typically drove separately wherever they went, even to church. At least one of the boys, usually both of them, was rushing off to their next leisure-time or school-related activity.

They seldom had family time anymore. Cooper missed the mornings when his father drove them to school, the conversations they shared about sports and current events, and the stories he told them about his patients. Back when he still drove the Volvo wagon. Before he bought this old man's wet dream. Cooper sniffed. The interior still smelled new, even though he'd owned the car for almost two years. The creamy leather seats cushioned him like a cloud.

He envisioned his parents taking off for a weekend in Beau-fort or Savannah next fall after he and Sean left for college, when their nest was empty and they were free to go as they please. He pictured his father peeling back the convertible top and his mother's dark hair blowing in the wind as she sang loud and off tune to songs by Aretha Franklin and Whitney Houston. Her, wearing those big round sunglasses that reminded Cooper of Flik from *A Bug's Life*. Him, with his Atlanta Braves baseball cap on to prevent his balding head from burning.

Thank goodness his mother would be riding shotgun and not that Daisy person.

Cooper rested his head back against the seat and tried to imagine his own midlife crisis. What kind of tricked-out vehicle would he buy? A red Silverado jacked up with mud tires—his deer dogs in a dog box in the bed of the truck and his rifles hanging on the gun rack on the rear window—came to mind. A truck so big he'd have to lift Annie onto the passenger seat when they went out to dinner. A vision of him driving his redneck machine down the crowded streets of Manhattan, surrounded by yellow taxicabs and big city buses, caused his daydream to come to a screeching halt. Maybe New York wasn't the best place for him after all.

There were plenty of Southern cities large enough to support lucrative careers in graphic design. Raleigh, Charlotte, Richmond. Even Charleston. He might survive New York for college, but he wanted to make his permanent home in the South. Closer to his parents. Next door to his twin. He and Sean would grow old together. Share holidays and go hunting. Serve as each other's best man when they got married and be there for each other when their children were born.

Cooper had realized a lot about the importance of family during the past week. And about the importance of love.

The caravan of Sweeney cars arrived at the hospital at the same time. They gathered on the sidewalk out front and entered the emergency room in single file behind Mike. The young triage nurse greeted him with a sympathetic smile and directed him around the corner to the elevators. No one minded being pressed together in the elevator. They were family, after all.

"Listen up." Mike held up his hand to get the group's attention. "Annie is already in surgery. That's all we know for now. I'm going to show you to the surgery waiting room on the second floor. A nurse should be in soon to give you an update. I'm gonna head back down to the ER and see what I can find out about Thea and her mother."

None of them asked questions, because no one knew what questions to ask.

Cooper found a seat in a secluded corner of the empty waiting room, away from his family. The day's lineup of college basketball games had ended and two commentators were offering recaps on the wall-mounted television nearby.

Sean approached him. "Can I get you something, bro? Maybe a Coke."

"Nah. I'm fine. But thanks," Cooper said, slumping down in his chair preparing for a long wait.

"Okay, then." Sean dropped to the chair beside him. "Let me know if you change your mind."

His twin's presence didn't bother him. Sean didn't need to be told that Cooper wasn't in the mood to talk. Tonight, once again, they were two parts that made up the whole. They'd been together since the beginning of time. The beginning of *their* time anyway, when they shared the same space inside their mother's belly. Their understanding of the other's needs was innate.

*Oh God, what if Annie is pregnant with twins?* Having identical twins wasn't genetic, but that didn't mean it couldn't still happen. Annie hadn't been to see the doctor yet. At least not that kind of doctor. No tests had been done on her, like that ultra-whatever test where they took a picture of the baby inside the womb. If Annie was carrying twins, they'd have enough babies to go around. One for Faith and Mike. One for Annie and him to keep for themselves. The absurdity of the idea brought a palm to his forehead. He would never separate his twins.

But wait. If he wasn't willing to give up one of his twins, why were they considering adoption for just one baby? Truth be told, he'd never been high on the idea of adoption from the beginning. He'd been concerned about the timing of the pregnancy, about the glitch it threw in his plans for college, but the idea of having a little Annie or Cooper running around had always appealed to him. Annie had been shot, taken a bullet to the back. That much they knew. What if the baby didn't survive? What if she didn't survive?

Hours passed, or so it seemed, but it was really only thirty minutes according to the clock on the wall on the other side of the room. A nurse, dressed head to toe in mint green scrubs, appeared in the waiting room. Her gunmetal eyes, the only part of her body visible, studied them over the top of her surgical mask as they gathered around her.

She pulled off the mask. "I have little to report at this stage. Annie has a team of surgeons on her case. They're still assessing the damage caused by the bullet. But her vitals are strong, which is a good sign. I'll be back when I know more." She hurried out of the room before they had a chance to ask questions.

No sooner had she left than Mike returned with Eli in tow. He wore a grim expression and a five o'clock shadow. Dark circles rimmed his gray eyes. Rust-colored stains covered his uniform shirt. *Blood?* Cooper wondered. *Could it be Annie's?*

Eli gave Sam a peck on the lips, and turned to Cooper. "I'm sorry, man," he said, gripping him tight. "I did everything I could."

## THIRTY-EIGHT

ELI

Eli drew away from Cooper and faced the others. "I know you all have a lot of questions, but first and foremost is our concern for Annie. She's a very brave young woman. She was shot in the back while trying to escape the Bells' home. She's in surgery as we speak. I trust you already know this."

Heads nodded around the room.

Eli continued. "Thea shared some of what happened with me. I'll let Mike speak to Thea's injuries in a minute. But I'm here to tell you that Annie endured a lot inside that house. She's going to need our support in the days, weeks, and months ahead." Eli paused, giving this information a chance to sink in. "Now, as for the others, Willie Bell is behind bars. He faces a host of charges that will send him to prison for a very long time. His brother, Tyrone, is dead. Burning in hell, I hope, for what he did to his sister's face."

Mike stepped forward on cue. "Thea has a broken nose and a fractured cheekbone. Our resident plastic surgeon is in with her now. Thea is a remarkable young woman. Her efforts saved Annie's life. She's a survivor. She will make it through this. Eli is right in that we owe her a huge debt of gratitude."

"What about Thea's mother?" Sam asked.

"Flora didn't fare as well," Mike said, concern etched in his face. "Frankly, she's in pretty bad shape. She was in a diabetic coma when they brought her in. They are doing what they can for her. Only time will tell."

Sam brought trembling fingers to her lips. "What's gonna happen to Thea if her mother doesn't make it?"

Eli hooked an arm around her waist. "I can't turn my back on that kid, not after what she did for Annie. And for Flora. I hope you're with me on this."

"Absolutely," Sam said. "We'll provide Thea with anything she needs, even if she has to move in with us. We have an extra room."

"What are Flora's chances?" Faith asked.

"Fifty-fifty," Mike answered, and launched into an explanation of the complications of diabetes.

Eli's cell phone vibrated in his pocket. He extracted himself from his wife and took the call from the chief out into the hall. When he clicked on the call, he heard loud voices in the background. "Chief, are you there? I can barely hear you."

"I'm here. Sorry. Let me step away from the crowd." The background noise grew distant. "There. Now. That's better. The bride and groom are getting ready to leave. All the women are in tears. You know how it is. My sister is a basket case."

Eli leaned back against the wall, and crossed his tired feet. "You should be throwing rose petals instead of calling me."

"I've reached my limit of mushy lovey-dovey stuff for the day. Besides, I've just gotten off the phone with Logan Pomeroy. He couldn't say enough good things about you. According to him, you handled the situation by the book. He complimented your talents and your leadership."

Eli smiled to himself. It was bittersweet to hear this praise. "Thank you, sir."

"I wanted to be the first to congratulate you, Detective Marshall."

Eli's mouth dropped open. "I'm sorry. What did you say?"

Chief Andrews chuckled. "You heard me, Detective. I don't blame you for wanting to hear me say it again. It's been a long time coming. Take the next two days off to spend with your family. But be in my office at nine a.m. sharp on Tuesday to discuss the responsibilities of your new position."

Eli removed the phone from his ear, double-checking the caller ID. "Are you offering me a promotion?"

"That's the idea, Marshall," Andrews said, his tone now irritated. "But if you aren't interested—"

"Oh, I'm interested, all right. Thank you, sir. Thank you very much."

"Don't thank me. You earned it. I believe in rewarding my men for their hard work. If I had listened to you from the beginning, we might have avoided this whole ugly situation with the Bell brothers." Eli heard muffled voices, and the chief came back on the line. "Listen, Eli. I gotta go. My wife is here with me. I'll see you on Tuesday." He ended the call and the line went silent.

Eli stared at the phone in his hand. *Damn.* He'd finally made detective. Kinda hard to get excited with Annie on the operating table, Flora in ICU, and Thea's beautiful face smashed to a pulp.

*If I had listened to you from the beginning,* the chief had said. Eli had a long list of what-ifs that would cause him sleepless nights in the weeks ahead. What if he hadn't gone after the Bell brothers in the first place? What if he'd made certain Tyrone and Willie were in the farmhouse before he ordered his men to bust up their party? He'd known there was a high probability the brothers were hiding out inside Flora's house. What if he'd forced his way in the first time he'd knocked on her door that afternoon? What if he'd waited in the driveway for Thea and Annie to come home?

He walked to the window at the end of the hallway and

stared out at the lights illuminating the sidewalks and parking lot. He couldn't very well go back in the waiting room and boast about his good fortune. He would keep it to himself for now. If Annie didn't make it, he'd turn down the promotion. No way could he wear the detective badge knowing his ambition, his desire for advancement had cost Annie her life.

There were plenty of other ways, safer ways, to earn a living. Maybe he'd go into business with Sam. They could expand the seafood business into other markets, open up satellite locations even. He could teach criminology at the local community college or go back to school and get a degree in substance abuse counseling. He had plenty of time to think about it. The most important thing tonight was Annie.

THIRTY-NINE

ANNIE

Annie woke long before she opened her eyes. She determined from the now familiar, floating-on-a-cloud feeling and the beeping of the heart monitor that she was in the hospital. She searched her mind for its most recent memories. What'd happened that landed her there? The car accident? No, that was ten days ago. Thea's house. Her evil brothers. Annie had tried to escape and the pressure from the gunshot wound. She wiggled her toes on both feet and then her fingers. Somehow she'd managed to escape being paralyzed twice in one month. Had the bullet hurt the baby? The bed began to spin beneath her and she opened her eyes. She was surprised and oddly comforted to see Heidi sitting in the reclining chair beside the bed.

Heidi saw that she was awake and smiled. "Welcome back, sweet girl."

Annie licked her parched lips. When she tried to speak, the words came out in a hoarse whisper. "Is Thea . . .?"

Heidi scooted the chair closer to the bed. "Thea is fine. The plastic surgeon patched up her face. Once the swelling goes down, she'll be as good as new. She's been asking about you. She wanted me to tell you that you rock."

Annie tried to smile but her lips hurt too much.

"She'll come see you as soon as she can. For now, she's with her mother up in ICU."

Annie swallowed. "You mean Flora's alive?"

"She had a rough go of it, but she's hanging in there. Showing some signs of improvement from what I understand."

"And Tyrone?"

"The SWAT team shot him when he tried to escape the house. He died on the spot. He got off easy if you ask me. Willie, his younger brother, is in jail. For a long time, according to Eli. You can rest easy knowing they won't be bothering you anymore."

Annie inhaled a deep breath. One question left. "What about the baby?"

She felt Heidi's hand on hers. "I'm sorry, sweetheart. The bullet missed your spinal chord by a fraction of a centimeter. You're fortunate that you weren't paralyzed, but the trauma to your body was too much for the fetus."

Annie looked away. Her *fetus* had never stood a chance. The tiny creature growing inside of her that she'd begun to think of in terms of gender and hair and eye color had never grown larger than a lima bean. "I'm sure Jackie's glad."

Heidi sighed. "To tell you the truth, she's heartbroken. She feels awful about the way she treated you. She'll apologize to you in person when she gets the chance. Everyone was too emotionally involved, but given time, everything would've eventually worked itself out. I'm convinced of that. The Sweeneys all love you very much."

"They do now. Because I nearly died. They didn't love me so much yesterday."

"Don't be too hard on them. We've all learned some valuable lessons in the past few days." Heidi stroked her arm. "The doctors have assured us that you'll be able to have healthy children one day. You'll have your baby. But when you do, it'll be on your terms, when you're good and ready. It won't be anyone's business but yours and your husband's."

"I'm glad you're here, Heidi." The words spilled from Annie's lips before she could stop them.

Heidi studied Annie's face. "You are?"

Realizing that she was, in fact, very glad her mother was sitting beside her hospital bed rubbing her arm rendered her speechless. She nodded. Why play pretend with someone else's family when she could have the real thing?

"You have no idea how happy I am to hear you say that."

Annie paused for a minute as she collected her thoughts. "I'm grateful to the Sweeney family for all they've done for me." She swiped away a tear. "Truly, I am. I don't know what I would've done without Faith and Mike these past eight months. But it's awkward for me living with them. I've tried. I just can't think of them as parents. I had a different relationship with Daddy than most kids. I was more of a parent to him than he was to me. Even more so after he got sick. Faith and Mike mean well. But they treat me like a teenager. And I'm not like most teenagers."

Heidi smiled, and Annie saw something of herself in her mother's heart-shaped face and full rosy lips. "You most definitely are not like most teenagers. You are wise beyond your years." Suddenly struck by the irony, she added, "What am I saying? You are wise beyond *my* years." She moved from the chair to the edge of the bed. "My offer still stands, if you'd like to come live with me. On a trial basis, if that makes you feel more comfortable. I know nothing about being a parent. We'll just take it one day at a time and establish our boundaries as we go. How does that sound?"

"No strings attached?"

"No strings attached," Heidi repeated. "You'll be seventeen in May. In another year, you'll be free to live on your own."

"I'm not sure I can wait a year. I only have to be seventeen to apply to culinary school. I'm thinking about getting my GED, and applying at CIA for next fall." She'd already thought about how she could earn money for tuition over the summer. And if it wasn't enough, she knew Mike would loan her the rest if she asked him. But she didn't want to ask.

"I'd prefer you finish up high school, but if that's what you decide to do, I have some money socked away for your education."

Annie experienced a surge of anger. For years, most of her life actually, she and her father had barely gotten by. And Heidi had been saving toward her college plan? "Thanks, but I already have some money saved. I'll work this summer, two jobs if I have to. The institute offers scholarships and financial aid, which will help. I'll make it happen somehow."

"We can talk about the logistics later. In the meantime, I have a summer job for you if you're interested. I'm expanding my business. I recently purchased a renovated warehouse. I'm opening up a gourmet shop in the front and using the commercial kitchen in the back for catering. I could use your help managing the shop and organizing events. I already have several weddings booked for the summer."

Annie blinked hard. She'd eaten beans and franks five nights a week for most of her life while her mother had been earning enough money to buy a building, start a business, *and* send her to college. *Let it go, Annie,* she told herself. *It's all in the past. She's offering you a place to live on a trial basis. If it doesn't work, you can bolt. No strings attached.*

"In that case," Annie said, "I'd love to apply for the job." She'd enjoyed planning Sam's wedding with Heidi. They'd made a good team. If nothing else, she'd have a productive summer, maybe earn enough for her tuition if she didn't have to pay rent. Based on the photo album, Heidi's portfolio, she stood to learn a lot from her mother.

"Consider yourself hired."

"Congratulations on your new business," Annie said.

"Thank you. One day, when you're ready, I hope you'll consider it *our* business."

———

Annie dozed back off to sleep while Heidi was still in the room. When she woke again, Cooper had taken her place in the chair beside the bed.

He brought the recliner upright. "Hey there, beautiful. How're you feeling?"

"Like I got shot in the back." Her lip quivered. "I'm sorry about the baby, Cooper."

"Me too." He moved to the edge of his chair, closer to the bed. "I've had a lot of time to think during the past twenty-four hours, and there's one thing I'm sure about—we would've made it work. Someway, somehow, Annie, we would've brought our baby into the world and raised it to be a kind and honest human being. But we didn't stand a chance with everyone pressuring us the way they did."

Annie gnawed on her lip. "They were pretty hard on us. No doubt."

"Especially my mother. She feels terrible for being such a bitch. But that's Mom. The fangs come out when she feels cornered."

"Remind me never to corner her again."

"Seriously." Cooper rolled his eyes. "I was wrong about a lot of things, Annie, even before I found out about the baby. I pushed you away because I wanted to be free to make choices about my future based on my career goals. But I was wrong. Being with you inspires me to work harder. What's the point in being successful if you can't share it with the girl you love? And I do love you, Annie. That was never in question. I know now that we can still have a relationship while we are chasing our individual dreams."

"I'm moving to Charleston, Cooper, to live with Heidi."

His blue eyes widened, "You are? Really? That's great!"

She stared at him. "That's not exactly the reaction I expected."

"Why wouldn't I be happy for you? You have your whole life ahead of you. That's a lot of years you get to spend with Heidi. Which will help make up for the ones you missed growing up. When we have our baby, and we will have a baby, Annie, a whole litter of them if you want, Heidi will be our baby's grandmother." He chuckled. "The free babysitting alone is something to consider. You and Heidi belong together. You're family. You might not have a conventional mother/daughter relationship, but yours will be one based on friendship. Which is better anyway, since we're about to be adults."

"That's where you and I are different, Cooper. I already consider myself an adult. Because I never got to be a child."

"I know, Annie. But maybe now, with Heidi, you can relax a little and let someone else be the responsible one for a change." He took hold of her hand. "Charleston is only forty minutes away. We can see each other all the time. I can crash at Mom's carriage house, and you have plenty of places you can stay here. We don't have to live in the same town to be together. We might not see each other every day, but we can text and video chat. It will give us practice for next fall when I go off to school."

Annie removed her hand from his and cupped his cheek, rubbing her thumb across his lips. Cooper was such a dear person —still a boy in some ways, already a man in others. She didn't know what the future held for them, but she looked forward to finding out. She was closing one chapter of her life and starting another. The first sixteen years had presented challenges most kids should never have to face. But these hardships prepared her for the real world. While she was devastated over losing the baby, she knew in her heart the timing was wrong. Cooper and Heidi were both right. They would have more babies, on their own terms, when they were ready. Having Cooper in her life, and a career that made her happy, and a grandmother—two, actually—for her children was more than she'd ever dreamed she'd have.

Cooper brought her fingertips to his lips. "What'd you say, Annie? Will you give us another chance?"

With a big smile and no hesitation, she replied, "Well, Cooper, I'd like that very much."

# A NOTE TO READERS

I am dedicating this installment of the Sweeney Sisters Series to you, my faithful readers and Women's Fiction Fans. I am humbled by your continued support. You brighten my day with your emails, Facebook posts, and continuous stream of tweets. Your appreciation of my work inspires me to work harder to improve my writing skills and create intriguing characters and plots you can relate to. We travel over hills and through valleys during our journey in life. The friends we meet along the way are the blue skies and flowers that brighten our days.

While I love Richmond, Virginia, my home for the past twenty years, I miss the easy-going way of the folks who reside in the Lowcountry. Writing about these quirky characters and their unique way of life is the next best thing to experiencing them on a daily basis. I love the beauty of the area—the marshlands and moss-draped trees—and the southern accents and local cuisine. While this is the last installment in the Sweeney Sisters series, at least for now, look for more from the Lowcountry from me in the months ahead.

I love hearing from you. Feel free to shoot me an email at

ashleyhfarley@gmail.com or stop by my website at ashleyfar-
ley.net for more information about my characters and upcoming
releases. Don't forget to sign up for my newsletter. Your subscription will grant you exclusive content, sneak previews, and special
giveaways.

# ACKNOWLEDGMENTS

I am blessed to have so many supportive people in my life, my friends and family who offer the encouragement I need to continue the pursuit of my writing career. I am forever indebted to my beta readers—Mamie Farley, Alison Fauls, and Cheryl Fockler—for the valuable constructive feedback, helping me with cover design, and promoting my work. And for my Advanced Review Team whose honest reviews and amazing support help me launch my new releases.

I wouldn't survive a day in the world of publishing without my trusted editor, Patricia Peters, who challenges me to dig deeper and helps me to make my work stronger without changing my voice.

A special thanks to Damon Freeman and his crew at Damon-za.com for their creativity in designing stunning covers and interiors.

A great big thank you to my family—my husband, Ted, mother, Joanne, and my amazing children, Cameron and Ned, who inspired me every single day. And to my friends for your continued support. I'm so very grateful to each and every one.

## ABOUT THE AUTHOR

Ashley writes books about women for women. Her characters are mothers, daughters, sisters, and wives facing real-life issues. Her goal is to keep you turning the pages until the wee hours of the morning. If her story stays with you long after you've read the last word, then she's done her job.

Ashley is a wife and mother of two young adult children. She grew up in the salty marshes of South Carolina, but now lives in Richmond, Virginia, a city she loves for its history and traditions.

Ashley loves to hear from her readers. Feel free to visit her website or shoot her an email. For more information about upcoming releases, don't forget to sign up for her newsletter at ashleyfarley.net/newsletter-signup/. Your subscription will grant you exclusive content, sneak previews, and special giveaways.

ashleyfarley.net
ashleyhfarley@gmail.com

Made in the USA
Middletown, DE
16 February 2018